Night Train to Laredo

When gambler Ben Garner steps down from the train at Chandler Crossing, he feels a rush of adrenaline. He has arrived at a famed poker tournament, renowned for having the biggest pot of cash up for grabs of any game in the area. The slick card player is determined to enter the game, no matter what obstacles Lady Luck may throw his way.

En route to his hotel, Garner is robbed. Desperate and confused, he is suddenly confronted by a mysterious and beautiful female named Molly Walker. Her offer of a large fee to act as her guard and travel with her on the night train to Laredo seems too good an opportunity to pass up. But is this luck, or misfortune?

Night Train to Laredo

Roy Patterson

A Black Horse Western

ROBERT HALE · LONDON

ISBN 978-0-7198-1653-6

Robert Hale Limited
Clerkenwell House
Clerkenwell Green
London EC1R 0HT

www.halebooks.com

LONDON BOROUGH OF WANDSWORTH	
9030 00004 4470 0	
Askews & Holts	29-Oct-2015
AF WES	£14.50
	WW15009028

Typeset by
Derek Doyle & Associates, Shaw Heath
Printed and bound in Great Britain by
CPI Antony Rowe, Chippenham and Eastbourne

Dedicated with pride to my son James. (BA)

PROLOGUE

The morning sun had barely lifted above the surrounding hills but its glorious golden light had already spread out across the vast landscape like a tidal wave. It washed over everything in its path and chased away the darkness like quicksilver until once again sunset prevailed.

Nothing escaped its brilliance or intensity.

As warm rays sucked the overnight moisture from the land a gleaming object chugged at a steady pace along newly laid tracks. The pristine locomotive had made good time as it headed along the gleaming rails towards the remote settlement of Chandler Crossing.

Clouds of black smoke and burning cinders billowed from its tall stack up into the cloudless blue heavens as its engineer and stoker ensured that it would reach its destination well ahead of schedule.

The muscular stoker dragged logs from his tender and threw them into the open mouth of the red-hot belly of the train's firebox. With the black cast-iron door closed the flames inside the box grew hotter and allowed steam from its boiler to turn the locomotive's huge wheels.

Nothing like the steam-snorting iron horse had been seen in this part of the country before. Engineering skills were progressing throughout the Wild West at a speed that most people did not welcome.

To those who had settled this part of the territory this was their land. A land which was not ruled by the faceless law created and set down in vast tomes back East, but rather by the barrels of men's guns.

For more than a decade they had lived by gun law, but knew that soon civilization would control them as it did all the other places it touched. Suddenly their entire way of life would be ruled over by men in beaver-skin top hats from back East. Men who had never set foot in their part of the country would grant themselves power over all who actually did live and work here.

Those who lived along the route of the rail tracks suspected that they knew why the railroad company had added a spur that deviated south from the original course.

Gold.

The soil here was full of the precious ore. That was the reason why they feared the coming of the Easterners. They knew that soon men would exploit their vast knowledge of the law and steal everything from them.

None of this meant anything to the scores of passengers who sat in their car and watched the vast panorama pass by the windows. They were simply enjoying the comfort of the journey, a journey that had not bruised their rumps or covered them in trail dust like wagons, stage-coaches and horses had always done. They would arrive nearly as clean as when they had set out. And on time, for the mighty locomotive had not slowed its pace since starting out on its maiden run along the southern spur.

Ben Garner stared out at the passing scenery with more than a hint of excitement in his youth-ful features. Soon he would arrive at Chandler Crossing and then he would play the game of his life. This was where the biggest and brashest of poker games were played and Garner just happened to be a gambler.

For more than a year Garner had been working towards this adventure and he was ready. He had his stake money and had honed his card skills like a barber sharpens a straight razor on a whetstone.

Ben Garner was ready to take on all comers.

As the sound of the locomotive's giant wheels rotating on track resounded inside the luxurious passenger car his nimble hands had been practising with the deck of cards he always kept in his silk vest pocket – practising skills that he would never share with his opponents.

Now, as Garner looked through the large pane of glass at the scenery they were travelling through, the morning sunshine revealed the scars in the hills that surrounded the settlement, the scars left by the hundreds of miners who had discovered the rich veins of gold hidden just below the surface. Garner knew that where there was gold there were always towns willing and able to offer the miners anything they wanted.

Fortunes were won and lost nearly every day in places like Chandler Crossing. Garner intended to win as much money as he could and then get out of the lawless settlement with all speed.

All he had to do was win.

It was a simple plan but the only one he had.

As the train gently rocked as it continued over the tracks, Garner stared ahead at the town which appeared to glint in the morning sunshine. The locomotive headed towards the newly erected rail head and its waiting water tower at a slowing speed.

He had resumed toying with the playing cards when a shadow crossed his lap and caught his attention. It was the shadow of a well-dressed female.

Garner looked up and took a sharp intake of breath. He was stunned by the beautiful sight he was looking at. Clad from head to toe in her finery the female looked as though she ought to be somewhere back East rather than here, headed towards a lawless town.

Molly Walker was certainly a handsome woman and she knew it. She rested a gloved hand on the high-backed seat and smiled down at the gambler. She pointed at the empty bench seat opposite him with her parasol.

'May I join you, Mr Garner?' she asked politely.

Her voice was like melted butter. It smothered

him in its glorious flavour.

'I'd be happy if you would,' Garner said before realizing that the beautiful woman somehow knew his name. He watched as she sat down and adjusted her exquisite dress, then he looked into her eyes. 'And just how do you know my name, ma'am? We ain't ever met.'

'Are you sure?' She glanced at the scenery.

'I'd never forget anyone that looks like you.' Garner smiled as he pushed the deck of cards into his vest pocket. 'How do you happen to know me?'

Molly Walker loosened the drawstring of her small bag and looked inside it. A smile crossed her face as she pulled out a small tin and opened it. She withdrew a two-inch-long cigar and placed it between her pink lips.

'You are Ben Garner, aren't you?' she asked as he pulled a match from his pocket and ignited it with his thumbnail.

He offered her the flame and watched as she inhaled the smoke. Molly Walker sat back and stared at him through the thickest black eyelashes he had ever seen.

'I'm Ben Garner OK, ma'am,' he said. He blew out the flame and dropped the blackened wood into a fixed ashtray by the window. 'And what's your name?'

'Molly Walker.'

Garner smiled. 'How do you know my name, Molly?'

She said nothing for a few moments as she inhaled the cigar smoke. Then she dropped it, still smouldering, into the tray beside the smoking match.

'I observed you back in Apache Hills,' she said in a tone that rivalled the smouldering cigar she had just discarded. 'I asked a few people and one of them knew your name. I believe he was one of your poker victims.'

Ben Garner raised both eyebrows and smiled.

'I think I know who you're talking about, Molly.' He shrugged before leaning forward. 'But why would a lady like you be interested in a poker player like me?'

Molly did not answer straight away. She tightened the drawstring of her bag and then levelled her beautiful eyes on him.

'Do you want to earn one thousand dollars, Ben Garner?' she asked. 'A thousand dollars in cash?'

His smile grew even wider. 'I've got more than a thousand dollars on me right now, ma'am. I'm headed to Chandler Crossing to play poker. I intend winning a whole lot more, so I thank you for the offer but I can't oblige.'

She seemed unruffled.

'I need someone to travel with me to Laredo, Ben,' she said. 'I need a man I can trust.'

'How do you know I'm trustworthy?' he asked.

'Female intuition,' Molly replied.

Garner leaned against the padded back rest and eyed her carefully. 'I'm sorry, Molly. I can't help you.'

'Why ever not?' she fluttered her eyelashes seductively. 'Don't you care to work for a woman? Does it bruise your masculinity? Is that it?'

'I just don't like working,' he admitted. 'I'm just going to play cards and then I shall travel on to my next game.'

'A thousand dollars for two nights' work, Ben Garner,' she repeated. 'Anyone would think you don't like the thought of travelling with me on the train to Laredo.'

Garner felt the colour in his cheeks.

'I'd like to travel with you but I've got plans,' he explained again.

Molly Walker smiled at him. 'I'll be staying in the best hotel in Chandler Crossing, Mr Garner. When you change your mind you will find me there, waiting for you.'

Ben Garner shook his head. She was as persistent as she was beautiful, he thought. He knew that succumbing to either trait would be dangerous.

'I won't change my mind, Molly.' He blushed.

'I'll be staying at the Gold Strike Hotel.' She smiled.

'I'm staying at the other hotel,' Garner bluffed.

'There is only one hotel in Chandler Crossing, Ben Garner,' she told him.

The train whistle blew and the majestic locomotive began to slow as it entered the outskirts of Chandler Crossing. Garner watched as the fascinating woman rose to her feet and steadied herself against the back of the bench seat. Her gloved finger touched his dark curly hair and she stooped until he could sense nothing but her perfume.

'I'll be waiting for you, Ben Garner,' she whispered seductively.

The gambler tried to keep from looking into her deep blue eyes. It was impossible.

'You'll be waiting an awful long time, Molly Walker,' he gulped.

She blew into his ear and then made her way

towards the end of the car as it came to a halt.

'I'll be waiting for you, Ben,' Molly Walker said again, softly, over her shoulder.

Garner leaned from the bench into the aisle and watched as her bustle bounced from side to side beneath the layers of clothing she wore so gracefully. The young gambler straightened up, loosened his collar and sighed.

He picked up his hat and small canvas bag from beside him and stood up. He trailed the beautiful creature along the aisle towards the door that led to the conductor on the footplate. The smiling man waited there to help passengers down to the ground.

Garner hesitated for a moment. For the first time in his life the young gambler wondered if playing poker might have itself a serious rival.

A beautiful young woman who would not take no for an answer.

ONE

The gambler noted that Chandler Crossing had about everything anyone with cash could desire. Everything, that was, apart from a sheriff or court-house. After watching Molly Walker have her luggage piled up on to the back of a buggy and heading off towards the hotel, which stood at the far end of the long main street, Garner bit the end off a cigar, and raised a match to the tip of the long rolled tobacco.

He inhaled deeply. The smoke felt good as it fil- tered between his teeth.

After being confined for so long in the car of the train the gambler wanted to get some fresh air into his lungs and stretch his long legs. He also wanted to put as much distance between Molly Walker and himself as he could.

With the cigar in the corner of his mouth, Garner left the railhead, which comprised a water tower and a small ticket office, and started to stroll into the heart of the town. As Garner walked slowly through the quiet early morning sunshine his gaze darted around every building he passed.

Most were either saloons, stores or thinly disguised whorehouses. A combination that any man who lived by his ability with cards approved of.

Halfway down the long street he saw the saloon he had been told about. The Lucky Dice was by far the biggest of all the drinking houses in Chandler Crossing. This was where the hard-nosed gamblers gathered. At least, that was the information he had been given by his friends. This was the saloon where regular poker games that amassed fortunes were held.

Fortunes to be won by anyone who had the guts and luck to endure the challenge of games which sometimes could go on for days.

Garner touched his hat brim, then walked on towards the Gold Strike Hotel. As he crossed the wide street he could see Molly Walker entering the hotel, with the buggy driver struggling along behind her bustle. Even from a hundred yards away the gambler could see that her baggage was heavy.

Garner, deciding to keep his distance from the woman, stopped at a small café. He entered and sat close to the window. He placed his hat on top of his bag and smiled at the elderly cook who walked towards him.

'What'll it be, stranger?' the weary man asked.

'Ham, eggs and coffee,' Garner replied. 'And a slice of bread if you have any.'

The man frowned. 'Sure we got bread.'

Garner interlocked his fingers and stared out at the quiet street. He knew that by the time the sun was directly overhead the town would look very different. He had been to miners' camps before. He knew that gold prospectors were a strange breed. They rose early and started either panning or digging. As soon as their pockets were full they came to the nearest town to have an assayer's office and turned their dust or nuggets into hard cash.

Then they started to spend.

As the aroma of frying ham and eggs reached his nostrils, Garner had already worked out that the Lucky Dice should be full to overflowing by the time it was noon.

That gave him plenty of time to book a room in the hotel, get some shut-eye and then rise refreshed to start gambling. He had it all worked out.

At least he thought he had it all worked out. The more he considered his plan to simply play poker, the more he recalled the strangely confident Molly.

Doubts began to fester in his mind as he waited for his meal to be cooked. He tapped the ash from his cigar into the small ashtray set in the centre of the table.

By the time his breakfast arrived and was placed before him, Garner had found that he could not get the image of Molly Walker out of his mind. There was something unnerving about the feisty female that troubled the gambler for some reason.

She had been totally convinced that he would accept her offer, pocket the $1,000 and accompany her on the night train to Laredo.

He looked through the window of the café towards the hotel.

As the gambler stirred his coffee he wondered how she could be so certain. If she was a poker player, Garner would not bet against her having four aces in her gloved hands.

TWO

A devilish grin stretched the scarred features of Sol Davis as he reined in and stared at the three equally unpleasant-looking men who sat astride their horses facing him. The narrow tree-lined gully was the only route to where Davis was heading, and as the rider steadied his mustang he knew that they would not allow him to pass.

Perhaps it was the gold fillings in the mouth of the lead rider's mouth that amused Davis. It might even have been the fact that the horsemen were staring directly into the sun as they stroked their holstered pistols.

Whatever it was, Davis was unafraid.

Men in his dubious profession never feared

death, for they knew that it could strike at any time. To fear the inevitable was to fear life itself. Death was the only thing any of them who hired their skills to those willing to pay their price, could guarantee.

Davis pulled down on his dusty hat brim and watched the trio of heavily armed men. His burning eyes studied their every movement as he tilted his head and noted that his long shadow nearly covered the distance between them.

Davis had an appointment and he intended keeping it. For the time being the three riders were preventing him from keeping that appointment, and that gnawed at his craw.

For all Davis knew the horsemen might have been honest, but everything about them seemed to scream 'bandits' to the gunman. He knew that this land was rife with them.

They were everywhere and moved across the long unmarked border freely to ply their trade and avoid the Mexican lawmen who seemed unable or unwilling to capture anyone of their breed.

A less knowledgeable man might have continued riding in a vain attempt to pass them. Davis stood his ground and kept his horse in check whilst his half-closed eyes continued to observe them.

The horseman with the golden teeth began to call out in a mocking manner. Davis did not understand one word that passed through his expensive dentistry.

He did understand the gestures though.

As his companions chuckled the noisy bandit kept indicating for Davis to pass between them. It was as if the bandit was daring Davis to ride between him and his two cohorts. Davis was not as naive as the Mexican horsemen believed.

The gunman grinned even more widely as he pushed his jacket over the ivory grip of his holstered Peacemaker.

Davis flicked the leather loop off his gun hammer.

'I'd turn tail and ride as fast as them mustangs can carry you, amigos,' Davis called out in reply. 'Unless you want me to kill you here, that is.'

It was obvious that the bandits understood what he had said. The expression on their faces changed. The golden teeth disappeared behind a black drooping moustache as the bandit absorbed the words.

'You threaten us, amigo?' the bandit growled.

Davis nodded firmly. 'I don't threaten folks. I got the gift of seeing into the future. All I see for you boys is death.'

The three horsemen glared at the defiant Davis.

'Big words, *amigo*,' the bandit said angrily. 'You threaten us as if we were stinking bandits.'

Davis nodded slowly. 'Turn and ride, boys. If you don't the buzzards will have themselves a real big supper tonight.'

'My name is Pancho Lopez, *amigo*,' the golden-toothed bandit snarled. 'These are my cousins. We will kill you if you do not throw your pistol away.'

Davis shook his head. 'Just try, Pancho.'

Suddenly the three men went for their guns. Davis swiftly drew his own deadly weapon with equal intent. Like deafening thunderclaps the air within the gully resounded with the noise only six-shooters can make.

Bullets erupted from the barrels of the guns. Smoke billowed out in both directions as tapers of venom carved a route through the hot air.

One by one the bandits were lifted off their saddles and thrown over the high cantles; bloody droplets trailed them from their high perches to the ungiving ground.

Their horses bucked and then galloped along

the gully away from the scent of death.

Davis sat astride his horse, holding his merciless Peacemaker in his hand. Smoke curled from his red-hot barrel and drifted up into the cloudless blue sky.

His gaze narrowed upon his handiwork as the dust settled around the three dead bodies. He tapped his spurs and encouraged his mount to approach what was left of the bandits.

The horse obeyed its master's every command and approached the lifeless bandits. When his mount was directly above them Davis halted and surveyed the results of his lethal accuracy.

His unblinking eyes stared down at the trio of corpses as blood trailed from the bullet holes in their torsos. The sun still flashed across the golden teeth of the open-mouthed Lopez: they dazzled like precious gems. When satisfied that the bandits were no longer any threat to him, Davis removed the spent casings from his smoking weapon and replaced them with fresh bullets from his belt.

'I tried to warn you and your cousins, Pancho,' Davis murmured, and sighed heavily as he returned the chamber back into the body of his smoking six-shooter. 'It don't pay to delay a critter in a hurry. I've got me a high-paying varmint to meet in Chandler Crossing.'

The determined hired gunman touched his hat brim in a silent farewell and looked out beyond the gully. Through the shimmering heat haze he could just make out the tin-covered roofs he had been heading towards.

He thrust the Peacemaker back into its holster and tapped his spurs against the flanks of his mount. The horse lifted its head and began to trot away from the mayhem that had just been created.

Sol Davis continued on his way towards the distant town as though nothing had happened in the gully. To him, nothing truly had. To the merciless gunman, killing vermin like Lopez and his cronies meant little more than swatting annoying flies.

He rode through the dusty terrain with only one thought on his mind. Someone willing to meet his high price had wired a message to Davis to meet him in Chandler Crossing.

Soon he would be paid his fee. Soon he would kill for profit again. Davis spurred on.

THREE

Scantily clad females mingled with the saloon's customers as they vainly tried to drum up fresh business before the late afternoon sun should set. But no matter how red-blooded the men were they had something else on their minds. Something that was far more attractive than satisfying their manly urges. Not even the bargirls' charms or their heavily perfumed flesh could draw any of the onlookers away from watching the last five card players as they fought it out to the last poker chip. They all wanted to see who would be the victor of the longest poker game yet to be played in Chandler Crossing.

The air inside the vast interior of the Lucky Dice only moved when some of its patrons walked through it. Otherwise the saloon was dense with choking tobacco smoke. Smoke which grew thicker the more the five card players seated around one of its central tables continued to play.

The five men had been whittled down over the previous seven hours from the scores who had originally tried their luck around the saloon at various card tables. As the winners of the poker games the five men all moved to the one table with their vast winnings and tried to collect the lucrative pot.

For the previous hour a few of the card players had been struggling as they slowly saw their stack of gambling chips dwindle away before them.

Only two men seemed to be getting the better of the marathon game. One was a stout figure called Klondike Casey who was known throughout the territory as being either a very good poker player or an experienced cheat, who so far in his short career had not been caught. Casey had more than $20,000 in chips at his elbow, and he intended adding to his tally.

The other player with a stack of chips almost as large as Casey's was unknown to nearly all of the other people inside the Chandler Crossing saloon. Ben Garner looked about thirty years old but in truth he was four years younger. He spoke with the hint of a Southern accent and dressed like a riverboat gambler. His long black frock-coat, silk vest and frilly shirt with a black lace tie seemed out of place in the otherwise rough settlement, which had sprung up when gold was discovered in the surrounding hills. Men in Chandler Crossing were rough, tough creatures who played as hard as they lived.

Garner seemed totally out of place but his genial smile and amazing ability at poker had earned him the respect of everyone who had encountered him since his arrival two days earlier.

Chandler Crossing was a frontier town in every sense of the word. It was young and most of its buildings were made from wood that had yet to lose its green hue. Some said that it would be gone before its paint had had time to dry.

So far the law had not found the remote gold town. So far neither religion nor civilization had slowed its pace as it galloped on towards its ultimate fate.

Nearly everyone who lived within its boundaries liked it that way. The men who toiled in the hills and along the riverbeds wanted nothing of the lives they had rejected, but all knew that soon it would catch up with them. It was an inevitable fact of life. Nearly every one of the people in Chandler Crossing prayed that they would be long gone before that happened. To most, the fleeting freedom of these towns was far more favourable than the alternative.

In the saloon room a fog hung just above the heads of the seated five poker players as they studied the cards in their hands.

Garner glanced around the faces of his opponents. The pile of chips in the centre of the table was now far bigger than it had been at any time since the marathon tournament had started.

It was a fortune and worthy of any pot to be found in the private gentlemen's clubs far to the East. Each of the players knew they had never been as close to so much money before and might never be in a similar situation again. To lose now would be a fate none of them cared to contemplate.

Garner realized that only Klondike Casey had the ability to prevent him from buying the pot. The young man placed his cigar down in the full ashtray, then expertly pushed a pile of chips towards the large pot. Casey's eyes flashed at Garner and his lip curled.

'You're confident, sonny,' Casey growled.

'I raise two thousand,' Garner said with a kindly smile on his face.

The three other card players could not compete with such high stakes and knew that the battle was now between Casey and Garner. They cursed and threw their cards into the middle of the baize. One by one they scooped up the few chips they had remaining, stood up and pushed their way through the spectators towards the bar.

Garner watched as they all blended into the crowd before he cast his eyes back to Casey. He raised an eyebrow and smiled at the well-known gambler.

'Looks like there's just you and me left, Klondike,' he remarked. He placed his cards face down and returned his cigar to his mouth.

Casey grunted and studied his hand.

If ever there was a man of whom it could be said that he had a poker face it was Casey. The man never seemed to show any emotion as he played one hand of poker after another. He had been angry at the start and looked exactly the same now.

He stared at Garner.

'I'll see your two thousand and I'll raise you five thousand,' Casey said drily.

Ben Garner watched the gambler as he slid chips into the centre of the table. He knew that Casey might only have a poor hand but he was willing to buy the game if necessary.

'I reckon this is getting mighty serious, Klondike,' he muttered thoughtfully.

Klondike Casey did not show anything but contempt as he glared at the gambler. No humour or any other emotion apart from his loathing for his solitary remaining opponent.

'It's your bet, Garner,' Casey said, glaring over his cards. 'Quit delaying the inevitable and toss them cards in. I got you beat and you know it. Every inch of you knows that, so admit it.'

Ben Garner smiled.

'I'm trying to figure out if this hand is as valuable as I thought it was,' Garner stated, and chewed on the end of his cigar.

Casey sat upright in his chair. 'Is it?'

'Maybe.' Garner exhaled and tilted his head. His gaze darted between the face of his opponent and his five cards. He had three queens, a five and a seven. He knew that Casey might have all the kings or even the aces. On the other hand he might be bluffing.

'Are you gonna bet, Garner?' Casey pressed.

The youngster inhaled on his cigar and then placed it back on the ashtray. He rapped his fingers on the edge of the table and reached for his chips.

Garner pushed two piles forward.

'I'll cover your five thousand and raise you another five thousand, Klondike,' Garner said, trying to look as calm as the burly man opposite him.

Casey nodded, shuffling the cards in his hands. 'You're trying to bluff me. I don't bluff easy, Garner.'

Garner had already figured that. He smiled and placed the cigar between his teeth.

'I figured you were trying to bluff me, Klondike.' He grinned.

Casey laid his cards down and stared at the youngster with eyes which seemed capable of burning holes in people. His knuckles rapped the baize.

'I tap you, sonny,' he drawled.

A bead of sweat rolled down his face, navigated his jawline and dripped on his shirt front. Garner started to realize that whatever cards Casey had, he was willing to risk his entire pot on their being the winning hand.

Garner looked at his own chips.

'I've got more than ten thousand in chips here, Klondike,' he said.

'I know,' Casey said blankly. 'I still tap you.'

Ben Garner rubbed his fingers across his chin thoughtfully as he considered the possibilities. He could retire and walk away with his chips, or he could risk everything and gamble at winning the entire pot, or he could lose everything.

Was Klondike Casey bluffing or was he actually holding the winning hand? The question burned into Garner's craw. He glanced at the stack of chips in the centre of the green baize. Garner knew that he might never get a chance like this again.

Without saying another word Garner pushed all of his chips to the middle of the table. It was the biggest gamble of his life. He sighed heavily and looked at Casey as the sturdy card player sat motionless in his chair.

Garner turned his cards over and fanned them out.

'Three ladies,' he said. Then he asked: 'What have you got, Klondike?'

There was a long silence. It seemed to last an eternity as Casey glared at the three queens. Then he shrugged and tossed his cards over his shoulder.

'Nothing that'll beat your hand, Garner,' he replied.

The Lucky Dice resounded to the cheering of the countless onlookers gathered around the pair of card players. It was a strange sound, a sound that Garner had never heard before. He stared in disbelief at his opponent.

'Nothing?' he repeated.

Klondike Casey smiled and rose to his full impressive height. He touched the silk-edged brim of his hat in salute, then lifted his silver-topped cane and tucked it under his arm.

'I was trying to bluff you, boy,' he conceded. 'Trouble is you didn't fall for it.'

'Bluffing?' Garner heard himself mumble in surprise.

'Sure I was bluffing, Garner.' Casey grinned. 'I figured that even if you had three aces you'd chicken out if I tapped you. I congratulate you on your nerve.'

Ben Garner sighed heavily and stared up at the impressive gambler, who was looking at the stack of gaming chips regretfully. The famed poker player grinned at the youngster.

'I'll be here again tomorrow,' he said.

'I won't, Klondike,' Garner replied.

'Good.' Casey nodded. 'Then I might just win.'

'You'll win, Klondike.' Garner smiled.

'I'm counting on it.' Casey turned on his heel and started to whistle as he moved through the crowd of onlookers.

Garner watched as the whistling Klondike Casey rested the cane on his shoulder and gracefully left the saloon.

Garner scooped the chips towards him and looked round to the bartender. He gestured to the tall thin man who sported a waxed moustache.

'Bartender? Cash me in.'

FOUR

By the time the bartender had calculated exactly how much Ben Garner had won and then paid it to the young gambler it was dark out in the streets of Chandler Crossing. Garner had himself a shot of whiskey to steady his nerves, then walked out of the Lucky Dice with more cash than he had ever imagined himself possessing even in his wildest dreams.

He paused on the boardwalk outside the saloon and surveyed Chandler Crossing carefully. Most towns grew busier with the coming of night, but now the lantern-lit streets seemed almost as quiet as when he had arrived just after sunrise.

Garner wondered why.

Quiet streets made him nervous.

Maybe the miners were exercising their other vices, he thought. Maybe they all liked to get early nights so that they might be able to start their hunt for more precious nuggets and ore early. Whatever the reason, Garner felt nervous.

He patted his coat front and felt the bulging wallet in its inside pocket. A hand-tooled leather wallet with more than $20,000 inside it. Garner glanced all around him and felt a cold chill trace along his spine. It had nothing to do with the temperature in Chandler Crossing.

For the first time in his short life he was worried about having so much cash on him. Actually winning was something he had never even considered whilst he played poker, but now he knew that every back-shooter must have heard the news of his profitable triumph.

In a lawless town like Chandler Crossing having too much money was like painting a target on your back. Garner could not see anything that resembled a bank along the wide thoroughfare, and that troubled him. It meant he had no choice but to carry his winnings around with him.

Then he recalled the beautiful Molly Walker and her bold request for him to travel with her for a payment of $1,000. Garner laughed to himself.

He wondered why she had wanted him to escort her, then he shrugged. Whatever her reason, he would never discover what it had been, he decided.

Now that he had this small fortune in his wallet Molly Walker would have to find someone less fortunate to keep her company.

He pulled a long slim cigar from his breast pocket, pushed it into corner of his mouth and struck a match along the porch upright. He puffed thoughtfully as he eyes continued to survey the quiet street.

After some moments Garner began to pace along the boardwalk. He moved slowly as he searched the shadows for any sign of trouble. Chandler Crossing being a lawless town, he knew that there was a downside to the freedom its inhabitants enjoyed.

Men here had no fear of the law.

The only law they understood was gun law.

Gamblers were always vulnerable when they happened to win. Garner had won the biggest pot of his entire life; now suddenly he doubted the wisdom of his choice of profession. A hundred eyes had watched his triumph. He wondered how many of those eyes belonged to back-shooters.

His elegant figure cut through the amber light that spilled from various storefronts and windows on his way back to his hotel. He intended to sleep until noon and then catch a stagecoach or train to the next town along one or other of their routes. As he continued along the street Garner paused every few steps, puffed on his cigar and listened for the footsteps of anyone who might be following him.

He looked at the many large glass windows on the opposite side of the street. It was an old trick. The windows acted like mirrors and allowed a nervous traveller like Garner to see if there was anyone dogging his trail.

There was no one.

Garner began to feel foolish. He had allowed his imagination to rage out of hand like a forest fire. It seemed that even in a lawless town like Chandler Crossing folks had a morality that many of their more civilized neighbours lacked.

The gambler looked through his cigar smoke at the Gold Strike Hotel, hoping that he would not bump into the feisty female again. He did not care to encounter her because it was difficult to argue with anyone as beautiful as Molly Walker.

The hotel was well illuminated by a half-dozen

lanterns hanging from its porch. Their amber light stretched out across the sand as Garner stepped down from the boardwalk and headed towards it.

For the first time since he had watched the bartender count out his winnings back at the Lucky Dice, Garner was beginning to relax. Nobody seemed to give a damn about him or the small fortune in his wallet. Apart from a few riders there was no one between Garner and his goal.

His renewed confidence had put a spring into his step.

He mounted the three wooden steps up to the boardwalk outside the hotel and reached out for the brass door handle.

Just as he hand gripped it he heard a faint sound, which stopped him in his tracks. Garner pushed his hat back over the crown of his head and listened again.

For a moment the gambler considered that the noise which had caught his attention was nothing more than a lovesick cat on the prowl. A chuckle had just left his lips when he heard another, more disturbing noise. Garner's expression altered.

It was no stray cat.

It was the pitiful noise of a woman frantically

sobbing, he told himself. Garner released the door handle and rubbed his jaw as he walked along the boardwalk to the corner of the hotel. He stared into the darkness.

No matter how hard he tried to ignore the faint sound of a lady in distress, he could not do it. Garner slid his hand to the shoulder holster hidden under his left arm. He withdrew the secreted .45 and stepped down from the board-walk.

Garner paused and listened.

This was more than just crying. This sounded as though someone was being hurt. The sounds of distress persisted. It was coming from the side street alongside the hotel. The young gambler looked up the street. Wherever she was, the shadows were concealing her from view.

He stepped forward.

Every instinct told Garner to take to his heels and make straight back to the hotel doorway. But he had always prided himself on being someone who never ignored anyone in trouble. Especially when it was a female.

A thousand thoughts flashed through his mind.

She might be the victim of a vicious attack, he thought.

She could be in danger of losing her life or, on the other hand, she might simply have tripped and broken her ankle. So many differing notions raced through the gambler's thoughts. Whatever the reason for her crying, he would never know it unless he found her.

He spat out his cigar on to the churned-up sand.

Garner gripped his gun in his hand and started to walk up the eerie street. The moon had not yet risen high enough in the star-filled sky to cast its illumination down into the small street.

There were numerous rickety buildings along the narrow street. With each step the sound of her sobbing grew louder.

Garner continued to pace slowly into the darkness. He swung the barrel of his gun towards every slight noise. Still there was no sign of whoever was crying – or of anyone else for that matter.

This part of Chandler Crossing appeared to be totally deserted. It was as if whoever had constructed the ramshackle buildings had abandoned them when they had accumulated enough gold-dust to erect better buildings.

He paused at a corner.

His straining eyes were becoming used to the

dimness of the street as he searched every doorway for the creature who had drawn him to this part of Chandler Crossing.

Her sobs had turned to screams. Blood-curdling screams. His heart pounded beneath his silk shirt as he realized that he was now closer to finding her.

With no regard for his own safety Garner ventured a few steps further on and then stopped at a narrow alleyway which cut between a pair of the abandoned buildings.

He could hear her more clearly now. She was close by.

Then Garner saw a shaking shape huddled on the ground.

Even the darkness could not conceal what he was looking at. Holding his six-shooter out before him, Garner moved into the alleyway cautiously. The closer he got to the small shape the more he began to sense that he had found what he was looking for.

A female was huddled on the sandy ground. She was whimpering now, like a whipped dog.

With no consideration for his own safety Garner rushed toward her. He had barely taken three steps before he felt the crushing blow of a gun barrel slammed across his head. He stumbled, fell on to his knees and looked through glazed eyes at the woman. Even in the darkness he could see her tear-stained face.

His gun fell from the stunned gambler's shaking hand as he reached out to her, as though he still wanted to help her.

Then to his utter amazement she wiped the tears from her cheeks and grinned at him. He watched as she rose to her feet and started to giggle as she stood above him.

Then another more telling blow came down upon his head.

It was like being struck by lightning.

A blinding white flash exploded inside his skull, then it was quickly replaced by a dizzying red mist.

Garner fell forward on to his face.

The gambler could taste the sand in his mouth but could do nothing to help himself. He tried to fight the waves of nausea that were dragging his every fibre into the unknown, but Garner was sinking into a maelstrom of swirling blackness.

No matter how hard he fought, Garner could not help but sink into unconsciousness.

He seemed to be tumbling into a bottomless pit.

His only thing that he was aware of as oblivion engulfed him was the mocking sound of the giggling girl. Soon even that faded.

FIVE

Much was hidden among the shadows of the lawless town as it lay shrouded in darkness. Some of its inhabitants were innocent enough: others carried the threat of future danger in their black hearts.

The sound of a trotting horse echoed around the wooden buildings for these who were out and about to hear it, but they were few. As the town clock chimed across Chandler Crossing to announce that it was midnight most of the townsfolk had either returned home or were frequenting the various houses of ill-repute.

At the far end of Chandler Crossing a dust-caked rider slowly emerged from the darkness and allowed his lathered-up mustang to walk to a long water trough that stood close to the entrance of the town's only livery stable.

This was on the poorer side of the gold town. This was where the miners who had yet to strike it rich boarded themselves and their horses.

Sol Davis eased back on his leathers. His gaze darted around the dimly lit area and was drawn to the heart of the settlement where many coal-tar lanterns glowed in the darkness of the night. The hired gunman could hear the sound of guitars and pianos on the night air. He dismounted with well-practised ease.

Like most of his profession he made little noise when he moved. He placed his hand on his gun grip and looked at the livery's high doors. They were wide open, allowing the stench of the horses out and the night air in.

The lethal killer left his mount to drink its fill and strode up to the doors. A glowing forge cast light of a satanic hue around the interior of the high-roofed building.

He remained by the door and called out:

'Anyone in here?'

For what seemed like an eternity Davis stood and stared into the livery. Then he heard the sound of hefty boots plodding towards him through the shadows. His eyes focused on the muscular blacksmith. The light from the forge reflected off his sweat-soaked face and arms.

The hired gunman watched the sturdy Gus Brolin as he approached.

Brolin glanced at the mustang and then at Davis. There was no hint of his thoughts as he sat down on a three-legged stool close to the forge and warmed his hands.

'Two dollars a day,' he grunted.

'Does that include feeding my nag?' Davis asked, keeping his hand resting upon his holstered gun.

'Yep.' Brolin nodded.

Davis turned and looked towards the unfamiliar town. He had never been here before but he had heard that it had plenty of gold and not a tin star in sight. Men such as Davis liked the idea of being able to slay without retribution. He stood tall above the seated blacksmith.

'I'm looking for a varmint,' Davis told the man.

The burly man looked at the hired gun blankly.

'Damned if I care, mister,' Brolin retorted brusquely. 'I tend horses. Folks just rile me.'

A smile appeared upon Davis's scarred features. 'Maybe the critter I'm looking for has himself a horse and you look after it for him, big man. Would you know him then?'

Brolin shrugged, then nodded reluctantly.

'Reckon so. There ain't a horse in Chandler Crossing I don't know, mister,' he growled. 'If the varmint you're looking for has a horse, I reckon I know him.'

Sol Davis scratched his chin with his thumbnail. 'Good.'

Brolin eyed the stranger. He did not like what he saw and made no secret of it.

'Who you looking for?' he asked.

'I'm looking for Marcus Wheeler,' Davis told the blacksmith as the giant of a man stared into the glowing coals of his forge. 'Do you happen to know him?'

Brolin reluctantly nodded again.

'Everybody knows the owner of the biggest whorehouse in town.' The blacksmith sighed heavily. 'You got business with him?'

'You might say so.' Davis looked at the bright lights of the lanterns that were lighting up the street. 'Where can I find him?'

Brolin stared at the holstered six-shooter strapped to Davis's hip.

'What kinda business you got with that pox

peddler?' he asked.

'Does it matter, big man?'

'Nope.' Brolin shrugged.

'Then where might I find him?' Davis pressed.

'Reckon he's where he always is, stranger,' Brolin said, watching the gunman carefully. 'He's in his real big whorehouse.'

'Where is this real big whorehouse?' Davis asked.

Gus Brolin lifted a hand and pointed towards the centre of the town. 'Down yonder. You can't miss it. He painted the whole building red. He even had the glass on its lanterns painted red.'

Satisfied, Sol Davis pulled two silver dollars from his shirt pocket and handed them to the blacksmith. He then added another five silver coins.

'That's for your time and trouble, *amigo*,' he said.

Gus Brolin looked at the unexpected coins in the palm of his large hand.

'I might have bin wrong about you, stranger,' he admitted.

'How'd you mean?'

'When I first set eyes on you I thought you were a back-shooting skunk.' Brolin grinned. 'Maybe you ain't.'

'Thank you kindly, big man,' Davis said through gritted teeth. He turned away from the forge. 'Give the nag some oats. He's plumb tuckered out.'

'He ain't the only one, stranger.' Brolin slid the coins into his leather apron and nodded at the gunman. He watched as Davis pulled his Winchester from its scabbard and then proceeded down the lantern-lit street towards the big whorehouse.

The blacksmith rose up and walked to the mustang. He grabbed its loose leathers and was about to lead the animal to a stall. He paused and looked at the gunman as Davis continued on his way into the heart of the town.

'Trouble,' Brolin grunted. 'That varmint is big trouble.'

SIX

The sound of an owl hooting somehow managed to penetrate the gambler's sore head. Ben Garner had no idea how long he had been unconscious as his eyes slowly opened. All he knew for certain was that it was still dark and his head was pounding like an Apache war drum. He blinked hard a few times in an attempt to clear the fog that blurred his vision. After the sixth attempt he managed to focus on the large moon which now cast its eerie light down into the alley where he was stretched out.

The owl swooped down and flew over the gambler. It had achieved its goal and awoken Garner from his involuntary slumber.

Stiffly, like a man three times his age, Garner

managed to roll over on to his side and slowly force himself up on his knees. He rested against the wall where he had seen the young whimpering girl huddled. Her mocking laughter still resounded in his pounding skull. His eyes searched for her but she was nowhere to be seen.

Garner recalled her tear-stained face as it had suddenly altered and started to laugh at him.

Even his throbbing brain was able to work out that she must have been part of the act. She had sobbed and lured a big-hearted fool into the darkness, where her accomplice waited to knock an idiot out cold.

He was the idiot who had had his head stove in.

Suddenly a thought came to him. Garner urgently patted his coat. The bulging wallet was no longer where he had placed it in the inside pocket next to his heart. Then he saw it on the sand. He picked it up and sighed.

There was only sand inside it now. Lots of sand and nothing else. He pushed the wallet back into his coat pocket.

His head was bursting. He raised a hand and carefully touched the back of his head. Garner winced as he found the two places where he had been clubbed. His fingertips were sticky as he lowered his arm.

He stared at the moonlit blood on the tips of his fingers.

Garner picked up his hat and six-shooter and clambered to his feet. Being upright made the gambler even more giddy. He rested against the wall until he had steadied himself, then he turned.

The walk between the Gold Strike and the alley where he had been attacked took twice as long as it had when he was searching for the sobbing female. Every step had to be considered as the gambler retraced his route back to the lantern-lit corner of the hotel.

The last time he had been so unsteady was on his twentieth birthday. Then it had taken nearly an entire bottle of whiskey to get him into this state.

Garner eventually reached the hotel and entered its elegant foyer. The brightly lit area only highlighted his condition to the only other person present.

The horrified desk clerk looked at Garner and rushed around the counter to assist him. The man gave the gambler some welcome support.

'Are you OK, Mr Garner?' he asked as he helped him to the desk. 'What happened to you?'

'I got my head busted.'

'Are you OK?'

Garner blinked and looked at the age-lined face. 'I've bin a lot better, friend.'

'Shall I help you to your room?' the clerk asked, trying to keep the gambler from falling over. 'Shall I?'

'I'd be mighty grateful.'

Garner kept his arm on the clerk's shoulder and both men slowly ascended the staircase to the landing.

'Where did this happen?' the clerk asked as he steered the gambler to his hotel room.

'Up a real dark street around the corner,' Garner sighed.

'But why?'

They had arrived at Garner's room.

'I got nosy,' Garner said as the clerk pushed a key into the door lock and opened it. 'It don't pay to get nosy in a strange town.'

The clerk helped Garner across the room to the bed. He eased the injured young gambler on to the mattress and then proceeded to light the room lamp. He lowered the glass globe over the wick and adjusted its brass wheel.

'Is there anything I can get you, Mr Garner?'

There was genuine concern in the clerk's voice. 'Maybe a sawbones to patch up your head?'

'I don't need a doctor.' Garner tossed his hat on to the bed and then lay down. Even the pillow hurt his pounding skull.

'This is real bad, Mr Garner,' the clerk said. 'In all the years I've worked here none of our guests have ever gotten themselves ambushed before.'

'Don't trouble yourself about it, friend.' Garner sighed. 'I'll just get some sleep and be right as rain in the morning.'

The clerk hovered over the gambler. 'What about a pot of coffee? I could rustle up a pot and bring it up here in no time at all.'

Garner looked up at kind-hearted man. 'That sounds good, friend. You go rustle up that coffee. It might clear my head.'

As the clerk made his way out of the open doorway Garner saw the unmistakable Molly Walker standing in the well-lit corridor.

She was staring at him silently.

'You gonna say something or not, Molly Walker?' Garner asked as he lay on the bed.

He watched her cross the room towards him. She was still wearing the expensive dress and fragrant perfume. She looked even more beautiful in the flickering lamplight.

'What happened to you?' she asked as she lowered her bustle on to the mattress beside the gambler.

'I got myself robbed,' Garner heard himself say.

'You got yourself hurt in the process, Ben Garner.' Her hands no longer wore gloves. He could feel her soft skin as her fingers gently touched his scuffed brow. She gently brushed the sand from his sweating temple.

He looked at her face.

It was so beautiful but he could not tell whether she was concerned about him or not. His head still hurt more than it had ever done before and he was unsure whether he was capable of reading her motives.

'Are you OK, Ben?' her voice was still like melted butter.

He smiled and went to hold her hand but she was far too quick for him. She placed both her hands in her lap and stared at him. He could feel her eyes studying his face.

'I'm fine,' he replied. 'My pride is bruised more than my head. Reckon I should curb my tendency to be gallant to strangers. It can be kinda expensive.'

'How much of your money did they take, Ben?' Molly asked.

'All of it,' he answered. Then he noticed her expression alter. 'Why'd you ask, Molly?'

She simply lowered her head and fluttered her eyelashes seductively. 'No reason, Ben. I was just thinking that maybe you'll reconsider my offer now. Now that you're financially embarrassed, that is.'

Garner looked up at the ceiling as if seeking divine guidance. He sighed and then looked straight at her.

'Who are you, Molly Walker?' he quietly enquired. 'Who are you really?'

Molly did not reply. She stood up, turned away from him and started back towards the corridor. He watched her bustle swaying beneath the fabric of her dress. When she reached the doorway she turned and looked at him.

'I'm in room six,' she said. 'My offer is still open.'

He blinked and she was gone from view. Garner inhaled deeply and propped himself up against his pillows. Her heady scent lingered all around him.

SEVEN

There was no name outside the red-painted wooden building but the scent of cheap perfume and sound of female laughter spilling from its open windows told Sol Davis that he had found the place where Marcus Wheeler was reputed to spend most of his time. The deadly hired gun rested his hip against a hitching rail with his repeating rifle's barrel propped against his broad shoulder.

Three horses and a mule were tied to the hitching rail behind his back, patiently awaiting their master's return. Davis had spent the previous five minutes observing the large building carefully, as if he wanted to know every inch of the façade for future reference.

He noted that its balcony stretched along the entire forty-foot width of the whorehouse. A set of steps to the right of the building led up to five windows. Davis calculated how long it might take for a man to climb out of one of the windows and descend the steps.

The burly blacksmith had been right about the lanterns all having their glass painted red. Davis bathed in their glowing light long enough for him to finish his cigar and then crush its butt under his foot.

Davis had seen enough.

His professional curiosity satisfied, he moved silently away from the scarlet building and made his way deep into the heart of Chandler Crossing.

Davis now knew where he could find Wheeler, but there were other more pressing things on his mind. He was thirsty after his long ride.

He rubbed his throat and glanced along the well-lit thoroughfare. He had never seen so many saloons in one street before. All of them were still open for business, just like the other buildings he passed.

Davis crossed over to one of the saloons. It was

a smaller, far quieter cousin of the noisier drinking holes and that suited the deadly killer. Davis did not want to draw attention to his presence in Chandler Crossing until his business was finalized.

There was no point in alerting his prey to the fact that there was a hired gunman in town. The victim would find out soon enough.

Without missing a step Davis mounted the boardwalk and pushed the swing doors inward. He continued walking to the long counter behind which an idle bartender stood. The swing doors stopped rocking on their hinges just as he placed a boot upon the brass rail below the counter.

'What'll it be, stranger?' the bartender asked.

Davis eyed the other half-dozen customers dotted around the saloon, then returned his attention to the man across the counter.

'You got any cold beer?' he asked, resting his Winchester on the counter between them. 'I mean real cold beer.'

The bartender nodded. 'Reckon our beer is as cold as you're likely to find in any of the other saloons, mister.'

Davis smiled and ran a thumbnail down the scar

on his face. He nodded. It made the bartender nervous.

'Fill a jug with it, friend,' Davis ordered. 'I got me a powerful thirst and it ain't getting cured talking.'

The bartender produced a jug from under the counter and placed it beneath a wooden keg. He turned the tap and stared at Davis as the amber liquid slowly filled the jug.

'Ain't I see you before?' he asked as he waited for the beer to fill the glass container.

Davis slowly shook his head and stared at the bartender.

'You ain't even seen me now, friend. I ain't never bin in this saloon and I ain't even bin in this town. You've never seen me. Savvy?'

The bartender went pale as he registered the threatening tone of the stranger's voice. Davis's eyes burned across the wooden bar counter at him.

'That's right,' the man stammered fearfully. 'You've never bin here before. You ain't even here now.'

Sol Davis smiled and glanced at the pitcher of beer as it was placed before him. He lifted a hand and dipped his index finger into the froth. The bartender twitched as he watched Davis slowly withdraw his digit.

'That's what I call cold beer, friend.' Davis said, and smiled.

EIGHT

Word of the arrival of the gunman had spread through Chandler Crossing fast. It seemed that prospectors were always interested in strangers who entered the gold town. A lot of other people besides the goldminers were also interested in Sol Davis's sudden appearance.

The owner of the Lucky Dice rested his hands on the rail surrounding his balcony and stared down into the long main street. Frank Dover chewed on his thick cigar and considered the news his spies had just brought him. Like all rich men Dover had surrounded himself with paid informants. They were his eyes and ears and nothing that either entered or left Chandler Crossing went unnoticed.

Dover glanced around the quiet street bathed in the amber illumination of countless oil lanterns as he puffed heavily on his cigar. He turned and walked back into his private suite set above the vast interior of his saloon. Dover lowered his hefty carcass on to a plush leather armchair.

He looked through the tobacco smoke at the two lean men standing before him. Tom Hands and Artie Snape were his hired help. The pair of failed miners did his bidding.

'Who is this critter, boys?' Dover asked.

Snape moved closer to his paymaster.

'We don't know, boss,' he admitted.

Frank Dover plucked the cigar from his mouth and looked at Hands.

'What about you, Tom? Have you heard what they call this critter?' he asked.

Hands shook his head. 'Nope. All I know is that he showed up on a real tuckered-out mustang and left the critter with Gus at his livery.'

'Gus didn't ask his name, boss,' Snape added.

'This critter did ask about Marcus Wheeler though,' Hands added. He was resting his hands on his holstered gun grips. 'Gus told him where he could find Marcus but he didn't go to the whorehouse. He went to the Bonanza and had himself a pitcher of beer.'

Dover filled his lungs with cigar smoke and sat brooding on the few facts his men had managed to gather concerning the stranger.

'What's this critter look like?' Dover asked.

'He's tall and lean, boss,' Hands answered.

Snape snapped his fingers. 'I just recalled what Bert the bartender told me, boss.'

Dover looked at Snape. 'What have you managed to remember, Artie?'

Snape crossed the room and looked down on his seated employer.

'He's got himself a scar.'

Dover looked up at the grinning face. 'On his face?'

Artie Snape nodded. 'That's right, boss. Bert said this varmint got a scar right down his cheek. Damn ugly by his account.'

Frank Dover rose to his feet.

'Sol Davis,' he said quietly. 'You just described Sol Davis, Artie.'

'Who the hell is Sol Davis?' Hands asked.

Dover walked to a table and picked up a whiskey bottle. He filled a glass with the amber liquor and then downed it in one swift swallow. He exhaled loudly and then turned towards his hired men.

Neither of them had ever seen Dover look quite so terrified before.

'Davis is a hired gunman,' Dover said.

'Like us,' Hands said pointing to Snape and himself.

The owner of the Lucky Dice walked between them and then paused. His gaze darted from one man's face to the others.

'Sol Davis ain't anything like you two,' Dover growled. 'He hires his gun out to anyone with the money to meet his fee. That varmint is the coldest killer this side of the Pecos.'

'We've done our fair share of killing, boss,' Snape said, toying with his guns. 'You know that.'

'Davis is a different breed of killer,' Dover told him. 'He ain't got himself a drop of mercy in his entire body. He ain't afeared of nothing and no one.'

'Everybody gets a tad edgy just before they have to kill someone, boss,' Hands said. 'They get afeared that they might be facing someone that's a little bit faster than them.'

Dover sucked on his cigar. 'Davis ain't got a fearful bone in his whole body, boys. He don't worry about getting killed because he ain't scared of dying. Most folks are smart enough to fear dying, but not Sol Davis.'

Snape shook his head. 'That ain't normal.'

Dover walked back to the balcony doorway and rested a shoulder against its wooden frame. He rubbed his sweating face and flicked the butt of his cigar out into the street.

'I want you boys to go out there and find out where he's staying,' he said, staring out into the moonlit street.

'I don't hanker after tangling with Davis if he's as loco as you say he is, boss,' Hands protested. 'We ain't crazy like him. We ain't got no hankering for dying.'

Dover looked at his men.

'Don't tangle with him,' he said. 'Just find out why he's in Chandler Crossing. Find out who has hired him and who he's come here to kill.'

'So you reckon he's here to kill someone, boss?' Snape gulped.

'That's right, Artie.' Dover turned and looked at his two men. He pulled out his wallet and gave them five ten-dollar bills each. 'Davis is here to execute someone and if it's me, I'd like some warning. Find out what you can, then get back here and tell me.'

'As long as we don't have to draw down on him,'

Hands said, ramming the bills into his pants' pocket. 'Bonus money ain't a lot of use to dead men.'

The hired men left the room, reluctance written in their faces. But they would do what he had told them to do.

NINE

The pot of black coffee had stopped the pounding inside Ben Garner's head but it had also made it impossible for him to sleep. No matter how hard he tried the gambler could not close his eyes for more than a few fleeting seconds. Everything he had experienced in the previous twenty-four hours kept returning to haunt him.

Every word he and the beautiful Molly Walker had exchanged in the locomotive as it neared Chandler Crossing echoed inside his mind.

Then he recalled the large pot he had managed to win in the Lucky Dice saloon, and how he had somehow managed to lose it all and get his head cracked open as well.

The tear-stained face of the young girl filled his

mind with a mixture of anger and sadness. Then the memory of her laughter grew louder and louder inside his thoughts. Mocking laughter: he felt as though it might stay with him for the rest of his life. A constant reminder of his total naïvety.

Why had he fallen for one of the oldest tricks in the books? Why? The question tormented him the more he vainly attempted to sleep.

How could he have made so many mistakes?

The soft mattress was no longer comfortable to the troubled gambler. Now it was also reminding him of how many stupid mistakes he had made in such a short period of time. He jolted upright, wiped the sweat from his face and dropped his feet to the floor.

He stared around the room.

The flickering lamplight danced upon the floral wallpaper.

Garner forced himself to stand. The pot of coffee had stilled the incessant war drums but he still felt the pain of the bruised skull that his neck somehow managed to support. He held on to the brass bedpost. He was still a bit shaky but a lot better than when he had arrived at the Gold Strike.

He straightened his long black frock-coat.

He walked out into the corridor and looked in both directions. Light from an open door cut a path across the carpeted floorboards.

Like a moth, Garner walked towards the light.

As he reached the room he saw the number 6 painted upon the door. This was Molly Walker's room, he thought. He was about to turn away when the door suddenly swung inward.

Her perfume enveloped Garner.

Molly Walker was standing before him in a silk garment unlike anything he had ever seen before. He imagined that this was what all well-bred young ladies wore when they were about to retire to their beds.

He was embarrassed.

'I'm sorry,' he said. 'I didn't mean to wake you.'

'You didn't wake me,' Molly said. She grabbed his hand and led him into the room. 'I was wondering how long it would take you to get here.'

The startled gambler was about to reply when she closed the door behind him. A bead of sweat trailed down his face as he watched her move to her bed. For the first time since he had encountered her, he could actually see her real shape beneath the silk drapes. Her figure was no longer concealed under layers of material, giving her the artificial shape all women from the fashionable levels of society favoured.

For the first time Garner could see the real woman. The silk was soft and seemed as though it were little more than an extra layer of flesh to his young eyes. He tried not to look at her but it was impossible. No red-blooded man could ever turn his eyes away from a sight so pleasing.

'So at last you have decided to accept my proposition, Ben Garner,' Molly said. She sat down and stared at a small table.

Garner cautiously edged towards her. He noticed the cards on the table.

'You like playing solitaire, Molly?' he asked.

'No, I do not,' she corrected, and she looked up at him. 'But I had to do something whilst I waited for you to make up your mind and come here.'

Garner was uneasy. He had never before been in a lady's room at this hour.

'I saw the light and—' he started.

'Shut up and sit down,' Molly interrupted. She pointed at the chair on the other side of the small table. 'We have to discuss our business.'

Garner raised both eyebrows. 'We do?'

Molly frowned. 'Yes we do.'

'Reckon we do.' Garner still did not understand

this beautiful creature. He decided the best course of action was just to agree with her. It would save a lot of time. 'Then start talking, Molly.'

A ravishing smile lit up her face.

She edged closer to the table and looked into the still confused features of the gambler. She pointed a finger at Garner and waggled it.

'I knew you'd come around to my way of thinking, Ben,' she said. She beamed.

'Yep, all it took was a head-pounding.' He grinned and tried to get comfortable on the chair.

'I'm willing to hire you and pay you one thousand dollars because I need someone trustworthy,' Molly explained. 'The first moment I set eyes on you I just knew you were exactly the man for the job, Ben.'

Garner raised his eyebrows. 'What exactly is the job, Molly?'

'You're riding shotgun for me.' Molly nodded. 'You will protect me and a certain item that I'm carrying. Anyone who starts trouble will regret tangling with you.'

Garner looked even more troubled. 'I don't like the sound of that. You reckon I'll protect you and this mysterious item you're carrying from thieves who might try and steal it?'

She touched his cheek tenderly. 'I do, Ben. I've got total faith in you.'

The gambler curled his lip. 'Are you sure you've picked the right person for this job, Molly? I couldn't even protect my poker winnings from being stolen from me a few hours back.'

'You were taken by surprise,' she said.

Ben Garner forced a half-smile. 'One of them robbers was a little girl, Molly.'

'Bushwhacking doesn't count.' Molly tried to dismiss his worries. 'This job requires cunning and the ability to bluff anyone who tries their luck. Your being a gambler makes me think that you must be an expert at bluffing.'

Garner furrowed his eyebrows.

'Hold on a minute,' he said. 'Just how do you know that I was bushwhacked? And how do you know that I was taken by surprise?'

She looked at the cards on the small table. 'News travels fast around here, Ben. The clerk mentioned it.'

'He did, huh?' Garner said.

'Of course he did, Ben.' Molly looked into his eyes. 'I heard the commotion when he helped you to your room. I asked him what had happened.

How else would I know?'

'Exactly. How else would you know?' Garner threw her question back at her.

'Everything will be fine,' she assured him.

The gambler shrugged and looked at her. 'Tell me something. What am I protecting, Molly dear? Besides you, I mean.'

She rose abruptly to her feet and rested her hands on her hips. Garner felt as if he were being scolded by a schoolma'am.

'Off to your room, Ben Garner,' she said, pointing at the door. 'I'll tell you the rest when we take the night train tomorrow night.'

Still no wiser, Garner stood up. He was about to leave the room, then he paused and glanced at her several times. Finally he decided to give up arguing with her. It was just pointless.

He was penniless and she was offering him enough money to stake him in a new poker game. However much Garner disliked the notion of working for his money, he was over a barrel.

Garner hesitated in the corridor as she closed and locked the door behind him. He scratched his jaw and was walking to his room when he heard a noise down in the hotel foyer.

Curiosity drew the gambler along the landing to

the top of the stairs. He rested his hands on the balustrade and gazed down at the hotel desk. The clerk who had been so concerned by Garner's injuries was staring at the latest person to enter the Gold Strike. He noticed the horror etched upon the clerk's face.

Garner moved quietly to one side of the staircase so as to remain unobserved while he took a better look at the stranger below his high vantage point.

The sight that greeted his eyes was not what Garner had expected. Sol Davis stood with his Winchester resting on his shoulder and his top coat pushed back over the grip of his holstered gun. Every inch of the hired killer oozed deathly warnings as he dipped the pen into the inkwell and scratched his name in the hotel register.

A sudden dread overwhelmed the gambler. Something deep down in his craw told him that he knew the new arrival, or at least knew of him.

The clerk turned the register and read the name that Davis had written.

'Welcome to the Gold Strike, Mr Smith,' he said.

Sol Davis pushed the brim of his hat back until the hat barely balanced on the crown of his head.

His eyes were narrowed and stared at the clerk, as though he were trying to work out how many bullets it might take to kill the man.

'How much do I owe you?' Davis drawled.

'Just one silver dollar, Mr Smith.'

Davis pulled a dollar from his pocket and tossed it at the clerk. He then waited for the room key.

'Room eight,' the clerk said, dropping a key into the palm of Davis's hand. He pointed up the stairs to the landing. 'It's the last door at the end of the corridor.'

Davis nodded and turned. Even from where he stood on the landing Garner could see the hideous scar on the gunman's face. He wondered where he had seen this devilish creature before. Wherever it had been, Garner recalled that the well-armed man had used a different name back then.

He also remembered that the stranger was reputed to be a hired gun. Men tended to die shortly after his arrival. Although nothing could be proved, it seemed too much of a coincidence to the gambler that this man and the other whom he recalled were not one and the same.

Garner watched as Davis walked away from the desk and towards the staircase. The gunman moved like a well-oiled machine. Every movement was lithe, like that of a cougar.

The gambler inhaled deeply and backed away from the top of the stairs. He turned and walked quickly to his room. He only just had time to close and bolt the room door before he heard the sound of the gunman's boots as he passed on the way to his room.

The sound of 'Mr Smith' inserting the key and unlocking the door of room 8 filled Garner's ears as he listened from behind the sanctuary of his own door. Then he heard the ruthless killer enter room 8 and lock the door.

As the gambler rested his back against his own door a chilling notion occurred to him.

Someone was going to be killed in Chandler Crossing, Garner reasoned. The heavily armed man was only here for one purpose. He would execute someone and then collect his hefty fee.

It was a sure bet. A certainty.

Garner could come to no other conclusion.

He moved to the bed, picked up his Stetson and placed it on his still sore head. He gritted his teeth and cautiously opened his door. There was no one in the corridor. Garner headed quietly for the stairs.

He descended and crossed the foyer to the desk.

'What name did that critter register as?' he asked the clerk, pointing to the landing.

The clerk jabbed his finger on to the large register. 'John Smith.'

Garner rested against the desk thoughtfully. He knew that there was no law in Chandler Crossing, but he felt that he should tell someone that a hired killer was in town.

But whom should he tell?

'What's wrong, Mr Garner?' the clerk asked.

'That stranger is a hired gunman, friend,' Garner told the man quietly. 'I've seen him before. He kills for money.'

Stan Gee had worked behind the desk of the Gold Strike for more years than he cared to recall. He had survived to the age of forty-one because he was always polite and never interfered in other folks' business.

'There's nothing we can do about it, Mr Garner,' Gee sighed. 'We must just keep our heads down and pray that he rides on out of here as soon as possible. It don't pay to be too curious. Look what happened to you when you followed your heart and didn't listen to your head.'

'That was different.'

The clerk shook his head. 'Listen to me and you might live long enough to take the train out of Chandler Crossing.'

Ben Garner knew the clerk was talking sense but something inside him refused to listen. He leaned closer to the clerk.

'Who runs this town, friend?' he asked.

'How'd you mean?'

'Even if Chandler Crossing ain't got any law it must have someone who calls the shots around here,' Garner said reasonably. 'Who do you figure is the most important critter in town?'

There was a long silence. Then the clerk looked at the gambler.

'There are a couple of real successful business folks in town,' Stan Gee said. 'Are they who you're talking about?'

Garner shrugged. 'I guess so.'

'The owner of the Lucky Dice has his finger in a heap of pies,' the clerk told him. 'They say he owns a few other drinking holes in town. He's pretty wealthy.'

'What's his name?'

'Frank Dover.' The clerk tapped his teeth and then added. 'The owner of the biggest whorehouse in Chandler Crossing is also mighty important. His name's Marcus Wheeler.'

Garner scratched his jaw. 'Do you reckon that either of those gents would be interested to know that they've got a fox in their henhouse?'

'You intend telling them?' the clerk looked a little taken aback.

'It's my civic duty, friend.' Garner smiled.

The clerk gave the young gambler a fatherly frown.

'Was it your civic duty to get yourself bush-whacked earlier, Mr Garner?' he asked. 'Sometimes it don't pay sticking your nose where it can get stomped on.'

Ben Garner cast him a pained expression. He knew the older man was right. His earlier gallantry had been painful and very, very expensive.

'Yeah, you might be right at that,' he admitted.

The clerk rested his elbows on the desk. 'Why don't you go back to your room and have yourself a real long sleep. You can get some rest before leaving on the train tomorrow evening with Miss Walker.'

Garner looked surprised. 'How do you know I'm leaving on the night train with Molly Walker?'

'She told me when she booked in here, Mr Garner,' the clerk replied. 'She said that she was leaving on the night train to Laredo with you.'

Ben Garner raised both his eyebrows.

'I've only just agreed to travel with her,' he said.

'Womenfolk.' The clerk chuckled. 'Ain't they just a mystery?'

Garner rubbed his jaw and glanced up at the landing. He was starting to wonder more and more about the lovely Molly Wheeler.

'Yeah, they sure are,' he agreed. 'Anyone would think that she knew that I was going to end up broke. How'd she figure out that I'd have to accept her job offer?'

'I don't understand.'

Garner shrugged. 'Me neither.'

The hotel door opened. Garner noticed the expression on the clerk's face change dramatically as he observed the two men who had entered the Gold Strike.

'What's wrong, friend?' Garner asked.

The clerk leaned over the desk and whispered.

'Them two *hombres* that just come in here work for that Frank Dover I told you about, Mr Garner,' he said.

The sound of the two men's arrival filled the foyer. They strode to either side of the gambler as they closed in on the clerk.

'Howdy, boys,' the nervous clerk greeted them. Dover's henchmen stood one on each side of the gambler.

'Howdy, Stan,' Tom Hands said as he reached the desk.

'You had any new guests tonight, Stan?' Artie Snape asked as he looked at the register. 'We're looking for a varmint with a real wicked scar on his face.'

The clerk pointed at the last entry on the register.

'That's the dude you're looking for,' he said.

Snape pushed Garner aside. 'It says his name's Smith, Stan. The critter we're looking for is called Davis. Sol Davis.'

'That varmint has got himself a scar, boys,' the clerk insisted. 'He must be using a fake name.'

'Where is he, Stan?' Hands demanded to know.

'Room eight,' the clerk told him. 'I'd not tangle with the likes of him though, boys. I ain't ever seen anyone who looks as deadly as him.'

Garner pulled a cigar from his coat pocket and placed it between his teeth.

'He's right, boys,' the gambler said. He struck a match and cupped its flame to the tip of his cigar. 'That critter looked meaner than hell.'

Snape and Hands glanced at the gambler as he puffed on his cigar. Hands turned to the clerk.

'Who is this dude?'

'That's just Mr Garner.' The desk clerk smiled. 'He had himself a real bad head-beating tonight.'

The henchmen studied Garner, then returned their attention to the clerk.

'Is Davis in his room?' Hands asked.

'He sure is,' the clerk told him 'He ain't asleep though, by my figuring. He only just went up there. I could mosey on up to his room and tell him you boys are interested in him.'

The henchmen looked at one another in horror as the realization of the potential danger dawned on them. Recalling the words of their employer filled them with trepidation. Garner noticed how the two men suddenly went pale. Without uttering another word they turned and marched back out into the street.

The clerk scratched his brow. 'Now why do you figure they high-tailed it out of here, Mr Garner?'

The gambler puffed on his cigar.

'It looks to me as if they didn't want to meet Sol Davis,' he answered.

Stan Gee nodded. 'Frank Dover must be curious about that stranger in room eight, friend.'

'I wonder why?'

Garner pulled the cigar from his lips and tapped its ash into a glass tray on top of the desk. 'Reckon I'll just follow those two and find out.'

'Are you a glutton for punishment, Mr Garner?'

'Reckon I'm just nosy, friend,' Garner said. He checked his secreted six-shooter, returned it the holster under his left arm and adjusted his frock-coat.

The clerk watched anxiously as the gambler walked slowly out of the hotel and disappeared from view in the street.

'I've never known a critter so darned determined to get himself killed as that'un,' he murmured and sighed.

TEN

The scarlet-hued building was still busy as its painted ladies plied their trade to satisfy the handful of prospectors who still had enough gold-dust left to spend. Marcus Wheeler had made his regular rounds of the large brothel and had returned to his private room at the rear of the establishment. The middle-aged proprietor looked exactly as anyone who lived off the profits his fallen angels generated tended to look.

When Wheeler had first arrived in Chandler Crossing as a young man, with a wagon filled with exotic females, he had been handsome and virile. Now he was a mere shadow of his former self. Time had taken its toll of the once envied owner of the most profitable whorehouse in town. Now

89

he was pitied as all creatures are pitied when they vainly attempt to hold back the passage of time.

His hair was obviously pomaded and his once muscular frame had turned into unflattering fat, albeit hidden beneath well-tailored attire. Yet Wheeler was far richer than anyone in Chandler Crossing could ever imagine, for he did not only own the red house but also nearly all the smaller brothels scattered around the mining town.

Wheeler still controlled his business with the same iron determination as he had always employed. That meant he would mercilessly have any of the girls maimed or even killed should they try to cheat him of his cut of their takings.

The sandy wastes surrounding Chandler Crossing were littered with the bleached bones of those who had crossed Marcus Wheeler. It was said that none of the females who had worked for him ever retired. They simply died, whether they wanted to or not.

To the sound of a clock's swinging pendulum he sat at his ornate desk and studied the books from his various whorehouses. Like a ravenous creature unable to satisfy its appetite he hungrily totted up the ever increasing profits.

Yet even with a virtual empire to control,

Wheeler only had three burly men to ensure that everything ran smoothly. Anyone who got on his bad side was swiftly and brutally dealt with by his well-paid entourage.

Sykes, Landers and Parkin looked as though they had all been cast from the same mould. Each of them stood well over six feet in height and was solidly built. They seldom spoke except to grunt at their employer when they had been ordered to do something.

The trio moved around inside and outside the red-painted whorehouse as they listened out for trouble. Apart from dealing with the occasional drunk none of the three men had ever had to do anything. What none of them knew was that this night would prove to be very different from all those that had gone before. For there was a stranger in Chandler Crossing and his name was Sol Davis.

Nobody knew who his intended victim was or who had hired him.

Everything seemed as normal to Wheeler. He closed his ledger, rose to his feet and moved across his office to where he kept his liquor. The sound of the numerous females either laughing or screaming out in feigned ecstasy penetrated the walls of his office.

Every moan they emitted meant more cash to the man who had lived off the immoral earnings of his endless supply of capable females.

Wheeler pulled the glass stopper from a decanter and filled a glass with whiskey. He had just raised the tumbler to his lips when he heard a different noise. It was one he was not used to and it alarmed the man.

He lowered the glass from his lips and stared blankly at his locked office door. Then suddenly a deafening blast shattered the lock and sent splinters showering over the stunned Wheeler.

The glass fell from his shaking hand.

'Sykes! Landers! Parkin!' Wheeler screamed out vainly to his men. Yet it was not one of his men who moved through the gunsmoke. It was the deathly scarred face of a man whom Wheeler did not recognize and its eyes were looking straight at him.

With his smoking six-shooter held firmly in his steady hand, Sol Davis grinned at Wheeler. Then the gunman's eyes speedily searched the room for any other signs of armed muscle.

There was no one else inside the office apart from Wheeler.

'Who are you?' the owner of the whorehouse asked fearfully. 'Who are you?'

Davis stepped over the debris-littered floor and glared at the wide-eyed man.

'Don't worry who I am. The question is who are you, old man?' he said, pushing the gun into Wheeler's silk vest and cocking the hammer.

Wheeler had never been so afraid before. He screwed up his eyes and tried to see his three men coming to his aid. No matter how hard his eyes searched through the smoke they saw nothing but Davis.

'Where's my men?' he screamed into Davis's face. 'What have you done with my men?'

With a ferocity few men could have equalled, Sol Davis pushed Wheeler across the room. The out-of-shape man landed in his chair as the hired gunman picked up the decanter and took a swig from its neck.

'I asked you your name, old man,' Davis snarled. He placed the decanter back down on a desk and trained his gun on the winded brothel owner.

'I'm Marcus Wheeler.'

'That's all I wanted to know.' Davis raised the six-shooter and blasted a single shot at the seated businessman. The back of Wheeler's head exploded in a hideous plume of crimson gore as the bullet passed through his skull.

Davis moved back to the doorway.

With smoke billowing from its barrel he cocked the weapon again and levelled it at the corridor. He had not expected to encounter any of the hefty men whom Wheeler had vainly called out to. Davis imagined that they were smart enough to know that their employer was dead and no longer needed protecting.

He had been wrong.

Sykes was first to appear in the corridor near Wheeler's office. The large man was toting a scattergun. Both its hammers were cocked in readiness.

Davis swung to one side as Sykes pulled back on both the weapon's triggers. The buckshot tore away large chunks of the wall, sending smouldering fragments of wood over the entire office.

Not giving Sykes time to reload his large weapon, Sol Davis leapt back into the swirling smoke and squeezed the trigger of his own gun. A red-hot taper of lethal lead erupted from his gun barrel and carved a route down the corridor. He heard Sykes groan as the bullet ripped into his ample midriff.

Davis did not wait for the large man to fall. He strode along the corridor, kicked Sykes's legs from under him and then fired another shot into the side of his head.

The deadly gunman continued on towards the front door through which he had managed to slip unnoticed only minutes earlier.

The joyous sounds that had filled the red building had now turned to hysterical screams as the calico queens began to realize that something very bad was happening.

The hired gun reached the front door through which he had entered only moments earlier. As his left hand gripped the brass doorknob he heard the sound of another large creature plodding towards him.

Davis swung round and saw Landers running through what he assumed was a waiting room. The big man had his gun drawn as he raced between the decorative furnishings towards the dishevelled intruder.

Landers fired his gun. The glass in the door shattered.

Then Davis pulled angrily on his own trigger and replied in kind.

Before the slivers of broken glass had landed on the ground at Davis's boots the burly Landers was lifted off his feet. Davis watched as a spray of bloody droplets spurted from Landers' wound.

Wheeler's hapless minder crashed through a table on to the floor.

There was no sense of panic in Davis. The gunman cocked his hammer again and fired another bullet into the middle of Landers' chest. A fountain of scarlet blood rose from the deadly wound.

Davis walked out into the street. The red lanterns that hung from the porch overhang cast a strange illumination over the hired killer.

He paused for a moment and shook spent casings from his smoking gun. He grabbed a handful of bullets from his pocket and inserted them into the hot chambers of his weapon.

'Hold it right there, mister.' A voice boomed out from the opposite end of the building's boardwalk.

Davis snapped his gun shut and jumped over the porch railing in to the well-lit street. As he landed a bullet cut through the air and took a section of wood from the upright beside his head.

The cold-hearted gunman narrowed his eyes

and stared through the smoke at the broad-shoul-
dered figure that was approaching him hurriedly.
Davis smiled.

It seemed too easy.

Parkin charged towards Davis like a bull attack-
ing the red cape of a matador. Davis stood his
ground and fired his gun over and over at the big
man.

Parkin staggered as one bullet after another it
him, yet he continued to charge. The man who
reached the hired gunman was as dead as the
others. Davis looked around and then decided to
disappear.

His work was done. He had fulfilled his contract
and earned his blood money.

Never taking his eyes off the street in front of
him, Davis walked backwards into the alleyway
next to the renowned whorehouse. With each step
he replaced a spent casing with a fresh bullet in
his smoking six-shooter.

Like all men of his evil profession Davis had
achieved his goal with the least amount of wasted
energy. As he reached the rear of the large red
building he turned and headed deep into the
shadows.

Not one soul had seen him leave his hotel

room. Not one soul would witness the cold-hearted Davis returning to room 8 at the Gold Strike.

ELEVEN

The sound of the brief but lethal gun battle had reached every corner of the town. The hysterical screaming, which continued even after the shooting had ceased, was even more chilling. Frank Dover walked out on to the balcony of his saloon and watched as frantic miners poured out of Marcus Wheeler's famed establishment and ran down the main thoroughfare. Dover glanced at the mayhem and suddenly knew that Sol Davis had something to do with the chaos.

Davis was in Chandler Crossing to kill, just as he had figured. The sweating saloon owner mopped his brow and was thankful that the shooting had taken place at the far end of town.

He gripped the wooden railing and then spotted Hands and Snape just as they were about to enter his saloon below him.

'What in tarnation is all the ruckus about, boys?' he yelled down at his henchmen.

The clueless pair looked up at their boss leaning over the railing. Neither had an explanation that would satisfy Dover.

'We heard the shooting as well, boss,' Hands said. 'It couldn't be nothing to do with Davis though.'

'He's over in his room at the Gold Strike,' Snape added.

Frank Dover glared through the lantern light. 'How'd you know that he's in his room?'

'Stan Gee told us,' Hands replied.

'Did either of you halfwits see Davis?' Dover pressed.

'Nope.' Snape shrugged.

'Then get your sorrowful backsides over to where the shooting was,' Dover ordered. 'Try and find out who done the killing and who done the dying.'

Snape looked puzzled. 'How'd you figure someone has bin killed, boss?'

Even the moonlight could not hide the fury and

fear which was boiling over inside Dover. He was shaking as he pointed.

'Quit stalling. Find out what happened,' he ordered.

Snape looked nervous on hearing the instruction. 'But there was shooting up yonder.'

Hands looked worried too. 'We might get ourselves shot as well, boss.'

Dover shook his fists furiously at his henchmen. 'I know. All I want you to do is find out who was doing the shooting and who got shot. Now earn that damn bonus money I paid you. Get going.'

Reluctantly the pair of half-hearted gunmen did as they were commanded and headed to where the gunsmoke still lingered in the evening air.

Ben Garner paused in the middle of the wide street and puffed on his cigar thoughtfully. He watched as the saloon owner marched back into his private suite while Snape and Hands reluctantly continued in the direction of the large red whorehouse.

The gambler remained unmoving as a half-dressed prospector staggered towards him. He raised a hand and stopped the terrified gold-miner.

'What happened, friend?' he asked the panting man.

'Some critter come into the whorehouse and started killing,' the miner gasped. 'I heard tell that old Wheeler got himself killed along with some of his bodyguards. As soon as the shooting finished we all run out of there.'

Garner allowed the distraught goldminer to continue on his way. He removed the cigar from his lips and frowned as smoke filtered from between his teeth. He looked back at the distant Gold Strike hotel, then returned his gaze to where the killings had occurred.

It had to be Davis, he told himself. Davis must have started earning his blood money.

But how could it be Davis?

As far as Garner was concerned the notorious hired gunman had achieved the impossible. Just like a skilled magician Davis had somehow managed to be in two places at once.

Instinctively Garner touched the hidden six-shooter under his arm, turned on his heel and started back towards the Gold Strike. He was walking as quickly as his bruised and aching body could manage.

Garner did not know why, but something was

102

telling him to return to the distant hotel. A trail of cigar smoke marked his wake.

TWELVE

The Gold Strike hotel, though impressively large, did not boast anything fancy in its construction. It was, like most of the buildings in Chandler Crossing, purely practical in design. There were no lights in the alleys that ran on either side of its facade, just ominous shadows. A sturdy ladder was nailed to one of its side walls, reaching up to the first storey. In all the years that the hotel had stood there, only one man had ever used the ladder.

Sol Davis moved from the shadowy darkness towards the side of the hotel at the speed that he had maintained since leaving Marcus Wheeler's large red whorehouse. The gunman reached the wall and looked up at the open window of his room. Ensuring that there was no one else in the alley the merciless gunman began to scale the well-secured ladder.

It was all part of his simple plan. If folks in Chandler Crossing thought he was in his room, then he had an alibi: none of the killings could be attributed to him. Davis had used a similar deception more times than he could recall. Only once had someone actually spotted him when he was earning his blood money. That had been in Waco and the man who had seen him briefly was a gambler.

As Davis climbed up the ladder towards his open window he tried to recall the name of the man who had nearly ended his lucrative career.

He had barely reached the ninth rung when he heard someone walking towards the front of the Gold Strike. He stopped and remained motionless as the figure of Ben Garner came into view in the lights of the hotel. Davis stared from his high perch at Garner crossing the street. The bright illumination shed by the hotel's many lanterns lit up the poker player's face.

Davis could hardly believe his eyes. The young figure that approached the hotel was that of the very man who had identified him back at Waco.

'Garner!' Davis hissed through gritted teeth.

The sudden urge to start shooting welled up inside the normally calm killer. It was the first time that Davis had actually wanted to kill someone without being paid to do so.

The deadly gunman heard the sound of unoiled hinges as Garner entered the hotel. The force of the hotel's front door being slammed behind the gambler vibrated throughout the building.

Davis rested upon his precarious perch for a moment and tried to gather his thoughts about the man he had just seen.

He was Garner all right. Davis was certain of it.

The blazing lanterns had illuminated the young man's features well enough for Davis to get a good look at him. There was no mistake. He could never forget the gambler's face.

It had haunted him for years.

Davis recalled how the handsome young man had told everyone in Waco who would listen that he had seen Sol Davis near to where someone had been brutally slain. It had been lucky for Davis that the hotel clerk had sworn on his Holy Bible that Garner must be mistaken, because Davis was in his locked room and had been there ever since his arrival in Waco.

Luckily for Davis the word of a trustworthy hotel clerk outweighed anything the gambler had said.

Yet even though Davis had been believed and allowed to ride out of Waco, he could not forget the keen-eyed poker-playing man who had almost managed to get him hanged.

Davis balanced on the ladder, rubbing the sweat from his face along the back of his sleeve as he fought to contain his fury. He was angry and wanted to teach the youngster a lesson he would never forget. The trouble was, Davis had not yet fulfilled his contract. There was still someone he had been paid to kill who was still breathing.

Davis slowly descended to the alleyway.

Every professional bone in the paid assassin's body ached as he stood in the shadowy darkness by the side of the Gold Strike. He knew that he had somehow to rein in his lust for retribution until he had completed his work.

But a fire was burning in his craw.

A raging fire that would only be extinguished when he had killed the interfering gambler.

The merciless killer intended to repay the gambler for all the trouble he had caused. Unable to control his anger a moment longer, Sol Davis pushed his coat tails over his gun grip. He descended the nine rungs of the ladder and made towards the front of the hotel.

Even though he was not going to be paid to do so, he intended to kill Garner.

As silently as a cougar tracks its prey, Davis stepped up on to the boardwalk and made his way to the double doors of the hotel. They were slightly ajar and Davis could hear two men talking in the foyer. Their voices were clearly identifiable as those of the clerk and the gambler.

Davis traced a thumbnail along the scar on his face and smiled. He would kill Garner and then kill the clerk, he told himself. It never paid to leave witnesses.

He was about to enter when he heard what the gambler and the desk clerk were talking about. The killer decided to listen before executing his feverish plan. Sol Davis paused, waiting as a vulture waits for its next feast to die.

'You're back sooner than I figured you'd be, Mr Garner,' Stan Gee said thankfully. 'I'm real happy you decided not to go look up Marcus Wheeler or Frank Dover. Them varmints would not be too pleased.'

'There'd have been no point in me going to see Wheeler,' Garner rested a hand on the desk and placed his cigar in the ashtray.

'How come?'

'He's dead,' the gambler answered, and added, 'I was told by a miner with his britches at half-mast that his bodyguards are also suffering from the same complaint.'

'Huh?' the clerk frowned. 'What you mean?'

'They happen to be dead as well,' Garner told him.

Stan Gee's face went ashen. He gulped and rested his shaking hands on the register, looking into the gambler's youthful facer.

'Who done it, Mr Garner?'

The gambler shook his head. 'Damned if I can figure that out, Stan. My first notion was that it must to be our friend in room eight but that's impossible.'

Stan nodded. 'It sure is impossible. That *hombre* ain't set foot in this foyer since he went up to his room. Reckon he's fast asleep by now.'

'I guessed as much.' Garner looked totally confused by the situation he had blundered into. His expression grew puzzled as he vainly tried to solve the mystery.

'What about Frank Dover, Mr Garner?' the clerk queried. 'Is he dead as well?'

Garner shook his head. 'Nope, he's still up in his quarters above the saloon. I saw him yelling to his men to find out who had gotten themselves shot. They didn't like it but they did what he told them.'

'Frank's on his lonesome?'

'Yep.'

'Frank must be real skittish about them killings,' opined the clerk. He produced a tooth-pick from his vest pocket and poked it between his teeth. The stick of wood rotated in his mouth as he thought about everything Garner had told him.

'I reckon he is.' Garner nodded. He picked up his cigar, struck a fresh match and puffed hard until he was satisfied it had rekindled. 'Come to think on it, Dover did seem real shook up by the shooting. I wonder why?'

'Maybe he heard about the hired gun in town,' Stan Gee suggested. 'Maybe Frank thought that he was the intended target and not Wheeler.'

'Could be.'

'Frank and Marcus must be the richest hombres in Chandler Crossing, son.' Stan Gee repeated his earlier words. 'Maybe Frank figures being rich might be plumb dangerous. Some folks will do anything to get their grubby hands on another man's money.'

'You don't have to tell me.' Ben Garner did not need reminding that having money could be painful. He rubbed the back of his head carefully.

Outside the hotel doors Sol Davis was grinning. The words seemed to rekindle the spirit of the deadly gunman as they penetrated his fertile mind. Davis moved quietly away from the hotel doors. His lips were stretched into a cruel smile. It was almost as disfiguring as the scar he bore. He walked down the wooden steps to the street.

There was almost a look of gratitude on Davis's scarred face as he checked his still hot six-shooter. The words that he had overheard meant that he could complete his task before sunrise without arousing suspicion. Davis had originally thought that he would have to wait until the following night before he could fulfil his obligation.

Knowing that Dover was still awake in his private quarters above the saloon while his henchmen were down the other end of town offered an even more tempting opportunity than killing Garner.

'Garner can wait for the moment 'coz I got bigger fish to fry,' Davis muttered as he paced down the wide moonlit street in the direction of the saloon. 'If Frank Dover is on his lonesome then I reckon I can finish the job I was paid to do tonight after all.'

Sol Davis headed towards the Lucky Dice. The infamous killer focused his gaze on the saloon as he got closer and closer. Lantern light spilled out from several of the buildings but the merciless slayer did not appear to notice any of them.

He only had eyes for the saloon.

As he strode towards it he noticed a set of wooden steps leading up to the balcony. The sound of a tinny piano being played filled his heartless being.

Davis had already worked out how he would get to where Frank Dover awaited the return of his hapless bodyguards. It would be a swift execution, he told himself as walked through the moonlight.

Swift and merciless.

THIRTEEN

The Lucky Dice was still open for business as Sol Davis stepped up on to its boardwalk and silently paced to the swing doors, where he paused and looked inside the large bar room. His gaze darted around the faces of the half-dozen chancers who still were somehow managing to drink and gamble the night away. Davis stepped backed from the doors before any of the saloon's wearying customers spotted him.

He strode to the corner of the building and began the climb up to the balcony. Each step was as silent as the last. Davis did not make one sound as he climbed to where he had seen lamplight spilling from Dover's private quarters.

It was as though he were a phantom.

Years of practice had honed this particular skill. It did not pay to advertise the fact that you were closing in on your chosen target. Not unless you cared for a bellyful of lead to greet your arrival.

Davis turned his head. There were a few men heading towards the saloon from the place where he had calmly executed Wheeler and his men. He had plenty of time, he told himself. Dover would be dead long before anyone reached the Lucky Dice.

The hired gunman walked along the boards towards the open doorway. Light shone brightly out from inside Dover's private suite and stretched across to the railings.

As Davis drew closer his right hand slid the .45 from its holster and cocked its hammer. He could hear Frank Dover inside the room. The man was pacing around his office like a nervous cat.

Davis stopped by the open doorway and stared in at the nervous businessman, who was filling a tumbler with whiskey from an array of decanters.

His narrowed eyes watched as Dover replaced the glass vessel's stopper, then downed the amber liquor in one fluid action.

As the fiery whiskey burned a trail down into Dover's innards the killer entered the room.

Dover had not heard a thing, he turned and suddenly saw the scarred face.

Dover placed the glass down on the desk and stared blankly at Davis. He saw the six-shooter levelled at him and tried to speak.

No words seemed unable to escape from the saloon owner's trembling lips. He watched, trying to think as Davis moved amongst the furniture towards him.

Davis paused.

'Is your name Frank Dover?' he asked.

Dover's gaze raced around the room as though he were seeking somewhere to hide. His handsomely decorated quarters offered nowhere capable of concealment.

'I am,' he stammered. 'Who are you?'

Davis grinned. 'I'm the *hombre* that's bin hired to kill you, Dover.'

The words chilled Dover. He tried to swallow but there was no spittle. His mouth and throat felt as though every drop of moisture had been drained out of him. His knees weakened and he fell backwards into a well-padded chair. Sweat trailed down his face as he stared at the cocked gun.

'Who paid you to kill me?' he croaked.

This time Davis did not answer.

Dover looked up into the scarred face. 'Why?'

'Nothing personal, *amigo*.' Davis pulled back on the trigger. A deafening explosion rocked the office.

Davis watched as his target jerked violently in the chair and a scarlet pool spread across his shirt front. The saloon owner frowned as blood trickled from the sides of his mouth.

Sol Davis cocked and fired his gun again. His narrowed eyes watched the destruction his second bullet achieved as it hit the seated man in the throat.

As the gunsmoke cleared, Davis returned to the balcony and headed back to the top of the wooden steps. He had just started down toward the street when he heard the sound of two raised voices.

Although Davis had never set eyes upon either of Dover's hirelings, he instantly knew who and what they were. Both men were running through the moonlight with their six-shooters drawn.

Davis paused when he reached the bottom step and glared at Snape and Hands as they raced across the moonlit street. He gritted his teeth and fired his gun.

Tom Hands was jolted as the bullet hit him dead centre and knocked him off his feet. The henchman appeared to lose all use of his legs as he collided with a heavy trough and tumbled to the ground beside it.

Artie Snape suddenly realized that he was now alone. He stopped and knelt as another bullet came from out of a cloud of smoke at the corner of the Lucky Dice. The hot lead passed within inches of him.

Then he saw the gunman leap over the handrail of the steps and vanish up an alley.

Snape got to his feet and rushed to where Hands lay. He crouched beside his motionless cohort and made as though to drag him on to his back. Then Snape's eyes narrowed at the sight that greeted them.

The lantern light beaming from the saloon showed all too plainly the bullet hole in Hands's chest, from which blood was still trickling.

'Damn it all, Tom. What you wanna get killed for?' Snape rubbed the gore off his hand and rose to his feet. He stepped over the body and moved to the wall. His heart was pounding. He glanced around the street. If there had been anyone on the street when the shooting started, they were

117

gone now.

He looked up. The lights from Dover's private rooms spilled out on to the balcony. The sounds of the shots that had drawn both Hands and himself back to the Lucky Dice still echoed in the mind of the bodyguard. He wondered whether Dover was still in his quarters.

'Maybe the boss can tell me who fired them shots,' he muttered to himself.

Without further thought Snape mounted the boardwalk and stretched to his full height. He clambered up the side of the saloon with an agility most grown men lose long before their whiskers start greying. He did not stop climbing until he reached the balcony of the Lucky Dice.

The scent of gunsmoke still lingered on the night air.

Cautiously Snape looped his legs over the railings and rushed to the brightly lit open doorway. He drew his gun and cocked its hammer. He spun round, narrowed his eyes and pointed the .45 into Dover's office. When the gunsmoke lifted he saw what was left of his employer.

For a few moments Snape did not recognize his boss. The blanket of crimson gore masked the features of the saloon owner. Then Snape noticed the clothing the lifeless body was wearing.

'Boss!' Snape ran across the room and stood over the remains of Dover. 'Nobody deserves to get themselves killed like this. Not even you, boss.'

The confused man holstered his gun and was about to turn when a thought occurred to him. He knew that Dover always kept a handsome sum in paper money in his wallet. Snape tilted his head and looked at the blood-soaked cloth of what had once been one of the most expensive suits in Chandler Crossing.

He cupped his ear with the palm of his hand and leaned over the brutalized corpse.

'What's that you say, Frank?' he joked. 'It's payday again? Well, golly gee. What's that you say? I can help myself? That sure is kind of you.'

Snape stepped closer to the carcass and carefully peeled Dover's coat away from the bloody shirt. Congealing blood, as tacky as molasses, covered his fingers as they slid into the inside pocket and retrieved the wallet.

The wallet was undamaged apart from being covered in Dover's blood. Snape straightened up, opened the wallet and gasped at the inch-thick wad of bills between its flaps. He had never seen so much money before – and it was all his.

Hastily, Snape's blood-covered fingers snatched the roll of banknotes from the wallet. He pocketed the cash in each of his pockets and then threw the sticky leather wallet across the room.

Again he wiped his fingers down the leg of his pants.

Snape looked at the pitiful body and touched the brim of his Stetson.

'Much obliged, Mr Dover.' He grinned, turned and walked back to the balcony doors. As he reached them he looked over his shoulder. 'Whoever killed you kinda done me a real kindness.'

FOURTEEN

A bemused Ben Garner stood at the hotel door with Stan Gee at his elbow, staring out at the moonlit street. Neither of them could work out where the latest gunshots had come from but both knew that somewhere in the town there must be at least one new cadaver to add to the killer's tally. The gambler rubbed his chin and looked down at the hotel clerk.

'Whoever was doing the shooting seems to have quit for the moment, Stan,' he commented. He tossed the remnants of his cigar at the water trough. 'Are you sure that Sol Davis ain't snuck out of here?'

'I ain't just sure, Mr Garner,' the clerk replied. 'I'm certain. Davis couldn't have passed me without my noticing.'

Garner bit his lower lip. 'You might have closed your eyes for a few seconds. That's all it'd take. He's pretty agile.'

Stan Gee shook his head.

'You don't need to have eyes open to know when that hombre is close,' the clerk explained. 'He smells real bad. Reckon he's bin riding for days and he's acquired the same scent, if you get my drift.'

Garner stared out at the quiet street. 'Do you reckon I ought to go take me a look around? I'm powerful curious. Besides, someone might need my help.'

'You lost your poker winnings trying to help someone,' Stan Gee reminded him. 'The next time you might not be so lucky.'

Garner touched the back of his head and winced.

'Thanks for reminding me,' He said.

The clerk shook his head wearily. 'Forget it, son. You've had yourself a real busy day. Go to your room and get some shut-eye.'

Despite himself the gambler started to nod.

'Reckon you're right, friend,' Garner conceded as they returned to the relative peace of the hotel foyer. 'There ain't no point in me poking my nose into this ruckus any further.'

'Now you're talking sense,' the smaller man laughed.

'Good night, friend.' Garner patted the clerk on his back.

The two men parted company at the desk. The gambler removed his hat and climbed the flight of stairs. The ascent made him realize that even if his mind was still alert his body was worn out.

He reached the landing and walked slowly down the corridor towards his room. By the time he reached his door he had removed his frock-coat. He inserted his key into the lock and had just turned it when the familiar voice of Molly Walker sounded in his ear.

'Ben,' she whispered.

The gambler glanced along the corridor. Her lovely head was poking out from her room. She appeared nervous and that seemed totally out of character for the usually feisty female.

Garner opened his own door, tossed his coat and hat into the darkness, then strode towards her. He was about to ask her what was wrong but she grabbed hold of him and hauled him inside her room before he had time to utter a word.

Molly pushed him against the door with unexpected force.

He raised an eyebrow and looked down at her as she pressed against him. Her perfume filled his nostrils as he gazed down at her beautiful but troubled face.

'Why, Molly,' he murmured. 'This is so sudden.'

'Quiet.' She looked slightly alarmed.

'What's wrong, Molly?' he queried, feeling her heart beating against his lean frame as she clung to him.

Her blue eyes were like pools of water as they looked up at him. She swallowed hard, then pushed herself away from the gambler as though she had suddenly realized that she had revealed to Garner a weakness in her armour.

Trying to control her emotions she walked back to her bed and lifted one of her tiny cheroots from the small tin on the table. She said nothing as the gambler studied her.

Molly struck a match and lit the cigar between her lips.

Garner walked up behind her, then stopped. 'What's the matter with you? You sounded kinda terrified. That ain't like you.'

'I apologise for appearing like a silly young

124

female, Ben.' Molly said. She turned and looked at the gambler; she had regained her composure. 'I'm being somewhat silly.'

Garner grabbed her shoulders.

'Something spooked you, gal. What?' he asked.

'I heard something outside my window.' Molly gulped and pointed across the room. 'It frightened me so I went to your room, but you weren't there.'

'Why were you looking for me?' He stared at her long and hard.

'I thought that someone was trying to break into my room and rob me,' Molly Walker explained. 'As you've probably gathered by now I am carrying something very valuable. That's why I offered you a thousand dollars to escort me to Laredo.'

The gambler leaned back and studied her. Every natural curve of her exquisite form could be seen under the silk dressing gown. He cleared his throat.

'I gotta say that you're doing a mighty fine job of hiding it, whatever it is, Molly.' He sighed.

'Be serious, Ben. Someone was out there.' She pointed at the window again. 'I heard him. I think that a burglar has followed me here to Chandler

Crossing and intends robbing me before I can deliver what I'm carrying to Laredo.'

Ben Garner made his way to the window. He pulled the lace curtains away and opened it. She watched nervously as the gambler poked his head out and looked along the balcony in both directions. She noticed that when he looked in the direction of room 8 he paused for a moment. She edged closer to Garner.

'Have you seen something?' she asked.

He nodded, straightened up and released his grip of the curtains. 'Yep, I've seen something, Molly.'

'What?' She moved closer.

'There's a ladder attached to the side wall of this hotel,' Garner answered, rubbing his jaw. 'The ladder leads right up from the street to room eight.'

She looked confused. 'Should room eight mean something to me, Ben?'

He shook his head and gently touched her chin.

'Reckon not, but it sure means something to me, Molly,' he replied. 'It means that I might have bin right all along.'

She looked confused. 'What are you talking about?'

'Don't worry, Molly,' he said gently. 'All you have to know is that the person you heard wasn't trying to break in here. I reckon he was using the ladder so he could leave his own room unnoticed. That critter has other things on his mind.'

'What sort of things, Ben?' she enquired.

Garner bit his lip and tried his best not to alarm her. It was not easy.

'If I'm right, the gent in room eight has bin killing folks in Chandler Crossing tonight,' he told her.

'There's a killer in room eight?' She pushed the small cigar into the ashtray on the bedside table and gulped. Her small fingers stroked her throat as she tried to absorb the knowledge Garner had presented to her.

The young gambler nodded. 'If I'm right, there sure is.'

'Why would anyone be killing folks in this town?' Molly asked fearfully. 'Is he a maniac or something?'

Garner pulled the six-shooter from his shoulder holster and checked that it was fully loaded. He reholstered the gun, then rubbed his bruised neck.

'He ain't loco, Molly,' the gambler explained.

'He's a hired gun. Folks pay him to kill for various reasons. A mighty profitable profession, I'm told.'

She sat down on the edge of her bed. Even horrified, Molly Walker was still the most beautiful female Garner had ever encountered.

'A paid assassin in the same hotel as me?' she muttered.

Garner moved to the door and opened it. She watched as he walked in the direction of room 8.

The gambler positioned himself to one side of the door, then rapped his knuckles against its varnished surface. He did not want to be hit by any bullets that might answer his knocking.

'You in there, Mr Smith?' Garner called out. He bunched his fist and knocked harder and louder.

There was no answer.

Garner returned to Molly and looked at her from the doorway. She gazed up at him from the bed. His information seemed to have taken the wind out of her sails.

'Lock the window and this door, Molly,' he advised her. 'Don't unlock them until I get back.'

She jumped to her feet and ran to him. 'Where are you going? Don't leave me alone, Ben.'

The young gambler could sense his sap was rising. 'Just make sure this room is locked up tight and you keep that lamp burning. That'll stop anyone from trying get in.'

She touched his sleeve. 'Where are you going?'

'I'm going looking for the varmint who is meant to be in room eight, Molly,' he explained. 'Don't ask me why 'coz I don't rightly know.'

'Stay here,' she pleaded.

The gambler raised his eyebrows and grinned.

'I'm not that kind of boy, Molly.' He winked.

After he'd left her she scowled. Then she remembered his words of warning. She quickly closed and locked the door and hurried to the window. She lowered then secured it.

She sat on the edge of her bed and sighed heavily for a few moments. She heard the gambler close and lock his own door and walk along to the top of the stairs.

'Something tells me that gambler won't live long enough to earn that thousand dollars,' she told herself.

FIFTEEN

The glowing red tip of a cigar lingered like a firefly beneath the porch overhang of a nearby feed store. It caught Ben Garner's attention as soon as he stepped down from the hotel boardwalk and started to cross the wide street. Garner stopped, pulled the brim of his hat down to shield his eyes from the bright moonlight, and stared straight at the dark porch. He could see nothing there except the glowing red tip of the cigar. The gambler took a deep breath, then walked towards the telltale sign that he was being observed.

With every step Garner took towards the front of the feed store he realized how vulnerable he was to anyone with a gun. It had taken his entire resolve to continue towards the cigar smoker.

Garner stopped when he reached the hitching rail and rested his left hand on its pole. He peered into the darkness beneath the overhang.

'You gonna stand there all night, Garner?'

The voice was unforgettable. Garner tilted his head and made his way to the boardwalk. He stepped up and looked down at the man who had addressed him. A silver-topped cane lay across his lap.

'What you doing up at this time of night, Klondike?' Garner asked the veteran gambler. The elegant man was clearly enjoying his cigar. 'I'd have thought that you'd be resting up for a new poker game.'

'I never sleep.' Klondike Casey removed the cigar from his lips just long enough to tap the ash from its tip. 'I plan my next game. I've bin sitting here for the longest while thinking about all the mistakes I made when I was playing poker with you.'

Garner shook his head thoughtfully. Casey was the finest poker player he had ever faced but, like all seasoned gamblers, he had become used to winning.

Garner leaned against one of the porch's wooden uprights and stared at the floor.

'You only made one mistake, Klondike,' he said.

Casey looked up at him.

'Just one mistake?' he repeated, a surprised tone in his voice.

'Yep.' Garner nodded.

'And just what was my mistake?'

Garner turned and faced the poker player. 'You were getting tired, Klondike. You had enough chips to keep playing for hours but you tapped me. I reckon you were so tired you got careless. You bluffed me when you should have folded.'

Even in the darkness under the overhang Garner could see the broad smile that spread across the older gambler's face.

'My mistake was trying to rush the result instead of being patient, Garner,' Casey admitted. 'You're right. I was tired.'

Garner moved away from the upright.

'Reckon I should have folded, Klondike,' he said.

Casey pulled the cigar from his mouth and watched as his youthful companion walked thoughtfully to the end of the long boardwalk.

'What are you talking about, Garner?' he asked. 'You had the winning hand. Why would you want to lose?'

Garner turned and grinned. 'Someone lured me into a side street, and that someone stove my head in, Klondike.'

'You were robbed?' Casey smiled.

'Yep.' Garner sighed. 'I took the bait and was reeled in like a dumb fish. Reckon I was lucky that I didn't get gutted as well.'

Klondike Casey stood up. He chuckled as he patted his young companion on the shoulder. He rested his cane over his shoulder and studied the street.

'I wonder who has all that money right now, son?' he mused. 'Whoever it is, I bet they'll be buying big until it runs out.'

Garner smiled. 'I should have been a little less gallant. I should have gone straight to my room and locked myself in there until sunup.'

Klondike Casey stepped down into the moonlight and stood still for a moment. Then he looked over his shoulder at the youngster.

'Where the hell are you going at this hour, boy?' he asked. 'You don't think that you'll bump into the varmint who robbed you, do you?'

'The shooting around town got me curious, Klondike,' Garner admitted. 'I've bin trying to figure out why someone would want the owner of that big whorehouse dead – as well as the owner of the Lucky Dice.'

Casey narrowed his eyes and stared through the cigar smoke at his young friend.

'You sound as if you have an inkling as to who done the killing, Garner,' Klondike Casey said. He looked closely at Garner. 'Do you know who the killer is?'

'I reckon I do, Klondike,' Garner answered. 'I have a notion the killer is a certain *hombre* called Sol Davis. I run into him a while back, but I couldn't work out how he could be in two places at the same time.'

'What you mean, Garner?' Casey pulled the cigar from his lips. 'It's impossible for anyone to be in two places at the same time.'

Garner raised his eyebrows. 'Is it?'

'Sure it is,' Casey huffed.

'I figured out how Davis does his killing and makes everybody think he's tucked up in his hotel room,' Garner said. 'Davis rents himself a room. Locks himself inside so everybody thinks he's getting some shut-eye, but he sneaks out the window and uses the hotel ladder to get out and back in again.'

'A pretty perfect alibi.' Casey grinned. 'If it's true.'

'It's true all right,' Garner insisted. 'That's what I'm doing out here. I'm trying to catch the critter.'

Klondike Casey frowned.

'A word of advice, Garner,' he growled. 'Don't try to figure out anything or prove Davis is the killer. Chandler Crossing is a town ruled by gun law, boy. Honest men die quick here. Head on back to your bed and get that shut-eye you promised yourself. Men like Davis don't cotton to folks getting too interested in their business.'

The gambler rubbed his jaw. 'You mean I should just forget all about it?'

'Exactly, Garner.' Casey touched his hat brim and started to walk casually down the street. 'You'll live longer.'

Ben Garner knew the advice was well meant. He watched as the elegant gambler strolled down towards the flickering amber lights still spilling out from the few saloons that remained open for business.

He searched his pockets vainly for a cigar. He looked about for some place where he might buy himself a cigar, then he recalled that his wallet had been stripped of banknotes. He pushed his fingers into his vest pocket and pulled out his last five-dollar gold piece.

The Silver Dollar saloon, standing on a corner, was one of the few drinking holes still burning its oil lanterns. Garner, catching sight of it, made straight towards its lights.

He had only taken three steps when a flash and the thunderous sound of gunfire filled the street. Garner froze in his tracks, then saw another blinding flash coming from the end of an alleyway.

Ben Garner felt as though he had been kicked by a mule. He was thrown tumbling ten feet across the sandy street and only stopped when he collided with a water trough.

The gambler tried to rise but his legs buckled beneath him.

Garner slumped into a crumpled heap.

SIXTEEN

There were two men in Chandler Crossing who knew that Ben Garner was no ordinary gambler like the thousands of others who had passed through the gold town over the years. One of those men was the notorious Sol Davis. The hired gunman had always prided himself on being able to kill anyone without ever being suspected. The other man was Klondike Casey.

As Garner lay beside the trough he began to realize that one of them had just tried to kill him. The shot had knocked him off his feet, but apart from his bruised bones Garner could not figure where he had been hit.

He was about to move when something told him to remain motionless on the damp sand beside the trough. He narrowed his eyes and stared across the street at the line of storefront windows.

Like a line of mirrors, the large glass-panelled facades reflected a great part of the street behind the spot where he had landed.

For a moment he saw nothing as his eyes cleared. Then a figure suddenly appeared from the cover of a dark alley and began to walk towards him. Even in his dazed state Garner felt as though he knew the man all too well. He blinked as his eyes strained to make out the figure more clearly.

He swallowed hard.

Whoever it was whose reflection appeared in the storefront windows was unclear to Garner. He remained totally still on the ground. All he knew for sure was that he was looking at the man who had tried to kill him a few heartbeats earlier.

Every aching sinew in his lean frame told the gambler that he must be glaring at Sol Davis, but as yet he still had not positively identified the chilling creature.

The smoking six-shooter in the man's out-stretched hand caught the bright light of the high moon. It sparkled like a precious diamond.

138

Garner realized that he had best play possum if he wanted to live a tad longer. He remained perfectly still as the gunman drew closer and closer. Sweat trailed down Garner's face as he waited for the inevitable second shot.

Garner watched the reflection carefully.

Then he saw the now unmistakable Sol Davis clearly as the deadly hired killer passed beneath a streetlight. Garner realized that the odds were now against him.

Davis might be the scum of the earth but he usually killed what he fired at. Garner knew he had been shot but could not tell where. He had landed so heavily on the ground that every part of his young body felt as if it had taken a bullet.

He wondered how much longer he had before Davis squeezed his trigger again and ended his misery. The hired gunman was still edging closer with the smoking six-shooter gripped in his hand.

Many times Garner had been described as a lucky man and now he knew it was true. Surviving Davis's first shot proved that Lady Luck was still favouring the card player.

Like a cunning rat, Sol Davis had taken a devious route around town on his way back to the Gold Strike Hotel. The unexpected and unplanned exchange of gun play with Dover's two hapless henchmen outside the Lucky Dice had caused him to be over-cautious.

His first plan had been simply to kill Frank Dover and then stroll back along Front Street. Exchanging bullets with Hands and Snape had meant that he could not risk being identified by the surviving bodyguard.

Davis had been intending to make his way to the alleyway alongside the Gold Strike hotel and climb the ladder to his room when he spotted Ben Garner meandering towards the saloon. Something inside Davis had snapped when he set eyes upon the unmistakable figure of Ben Garner.

Disregarding every rule that he had prided himself on keeping over the years, he had lost all reason. The usually emotionless gunman had succumbed to temptation and fired at Garner.

It did not matter one bit to Davis that he was trying to kill someone for free. All he wanted to do was repay Garner for almost getting him hanged. Davis had always managed to eliminate the witnesses to his outrages. He had killed them all. All, apart from the young Garner.

He had watched as the gambler was knocked off his feet, tumbled across the sand and crashed into the water trough close to the Silver Dollar.

Normally he would have turned and walked away after firing his gun. There had been a time when his first shot had always been fatal, but that had changed lately.

It seemed that his once perfect marksmanship could no longer be guaranteed to kill. He recalled how Frank Dover had required a second bullet to end his misery. As he strode silently towards the gambler, something told his vengeful mind that Garner might not be dead.

The poker player had not moved since he had been abruptly stopped by the water trough, but Davis was too old and wise to be fooled so easily.

Davis had to be certain.

The fiery rage inside him had to be extinguished.

Davis lowered his head and kept moving silently towards the crumpled figure lying in the shadow of the water trough. His eyes were burning as he focused all his hatred upon the helpless gambler.

He cocked the hammer of his weapon again.

The gleaming gun was trained upon Garner as though daring the gambler to move. This was the ultimate bluff, Davis thought. How brave was the poker player when the pot just happened to be his life?

How long could anyone remain motionless when facing a man with his gun aimed at him? That kind of resolve took courage and that was one thing professional poker players were shy of.

Each step was as quiet as the last. Davis homed in on his target with a relentless determination that belied his usually cautious attitude to his work. He no longer cared if anyone saw him finish off the gambler. The sheer joy of killing Garner outweighed all other considerations.

Davis stopped twenty feet from where Garner lay.

The motionless gambler stared at the gunman's reflection in the storefronts. His mind raced as he searched for a way out of the situation he found himself in.

All Garner could think of was the gun under his left arm in its shoulder holster. Could he draw the weapon, turn and shoot it faster than Davis could aim and fire his own gun?

Garner doubted that anyone could have done it.

Never taking his eyes off the reflected image of Davis as the ruthless hired killer aimed his gun across the distance between them, Garner managed to free his right arm from under his torso.

Davis could not have noticed the slight movement, Garner told himself. If he had he would have pulled on his trigger.

Garner's fingers flexed as they attempted to find his secreted gun. He never once took his eyes off Davis's reflected image as the brutal killer raised his gun hand to shoulder height and stared along the barrel's length at his victim.

There was no more time to think, Garner thought. He had to act now before Sol Davis fired again. Nobody of Davis's reputation could possibly miss from the distance now between them.

Summoning every last scrap of his courage and dwindling strength, Garner rolled over on to his back and hauled the six-shooter clear of its holster. At the very same moment Davis squeezed his trigger.

Garner felt the heat of the lead ball as Davis's bullet burned through his frock-coat. Yet the gambler was still somehow alive. He cocked and fired his own gun. Red-hot tapers sped through the moonlight in both directions and clouds of gunsmoke enveloped both adversaries.

The gambler rolled across the sandy ground when he had fired all the shots in his .45. He scrambled round the trough and huddled behind it as his shaking hands emptied the casings from his smoking gun and then searched his coat pocket for fresh bullets.

A chunk of wood was ripped from the edge of the trough and sent showers of burning splinters over the terrified gambler. As he forced bullets into the chambers of his gun he glanced around the smoke-filled air surrounding his hiding-place. The glowing splinters looked like a herd of fire-flies.

Garner snapped the chamber back into the body of the gun and locked its ramrod into position. He was panting like an ancient hound dog after a raccoon hunt as he forced himself on to his knees and peered round the side of the trough.

'You still alive, Garner?' Davis yelled out as he too reloaded his six-shooter and spun its chamber.

Garner did not reply. He knew that Davis was trying to figure out exactly where he was hiding. The gambler had no intention of making this any easier for the gunman.

Deciding that he needed cover, Davis ran to the saloon's boardwalk and knelt behind a large water barrel close to the corner. The cold eyes of the gunman remained fixed on the smoke-filled street. They searched for the young gambler as an eagle on a warm thermal seeks its prey.

'Where are you?' Davis shouted into the moon-light. 'Show yourself and fight like a man, Garner.'

Suddenly both men blindly fired their guns from the cover of their hiding-places. The eerie light was cut apart as a dozen vicious spears of hot lead carved through the night air in both directions.

Garner pulled the last few bullets from his coat pocket and forced them into the smoking .45.

'This ain't going to plan,' he muttered. The knowledge that he only had three bullets remain-ing troubled the gambler. He was sure that Davis would never risk running out of shells.

More shots passed over Garner's head as the merciless killer kept him trapped behind the trough. The gambler carefully clicked the chamber of his weapon so that its hammer would fall on his last trio of bullets.

Trapped, Garner knelt with the gun in one hand and stared at the other. The moonlight cast its glowing illumination on the blood that covered it. His coat sleeve had a savage tear in its expensive fabric just above his elbow.

The gambler pulled the ripped material away and stared at the graze on his upper arm. He flexed his fingers. There was no pain.

'You still out there?' Garner shouted at the top of his voice.

'I'm still here, Garner,' Davis yelled back. 'Pretty soon I'll be on my lonesome. You'll be dead.'

'I wouldn't bet against that, Davis.' The gambler sighed knowing that he had just three bullets between himself and death. Nervously, Garner peered around the side of the trough in a vain search for the deadly slayer. No matter how hard he tried he could not see anything beyond the lantern lights of the Silver Dollar saloon. Their bright illumination made it impossible to make anything out clearly. The gentle night breeze blew the gunsmoke from the street. It was like observing the spirits of fallen men floating upward in the moonlight.

Davis had heard the sound of defeat in the gambler's shaky voice and that encouraged him. He was only twenty feet away from his prey and he knew that Garner was trapped. There was no way Garner could escape his fate.

With the scent of the gambler's spilled blood in his nostrils, Davis stood behind the water barrel with his gun held in his outstretched arm. He cocked the hammer of his smoking weapon and levelled its sights at the rim of the trough.

His finger curled around the trigger, Sol Davis closed one eye and took aim.

'Show your yellow hide, Garner,' he screamed out.

Ben Garner continued to look towards the lights of the saloon. He could just make out the silhouette of the venomous hired killer who was trying to taunt him away from the bullet-ridden trough.

Garner narrowed his eyes and squinted. The lanterns in the saloon glowed brightly. The pools of coal tar light dazzled and confused the gambler. He would have attempted to shoot out the lanterns if he'd had more ammunition.

The trouble was Garner was not convinced that his three remaining bullets were enough to stop Davis. The card player had never shot anyone in his life, unlike the man who seemed determined to kill him. Garner had never had his skill tested when it came to gun play.

As he stood behind the large wooden barrel a movement caught Davis's attention. The hired killer swung to his left and aimed his weapon at the hardware store's dark porch.

For a seemingly endless moment he saw nothing. Davis gripped the gun in his hand and narrowed his eyes. His finger stroked the trigger in readiness to send another soul to Boot Hill.

Then suddenly Davis saw the scarlet tip of a cigar. It glowed in the blackness beneath the store's porch overhang as the unseen observer watched the two men in their desperate duel.

'Show yourself!' Davis snarled.

Klondike Casey emerged into the moonlight, his cane resting on his shoulder. The veteran gambler stood on the edge of the boardwalk and silently continued to watch Davis and the crouching Garner.

Garner could not believe his eyes.

'Take cover, Klondike,' he warned. 'That's Sol Davis. He's a deadly killer.'

Casey did not seem even to flinch. It was as if the information meant nothing to him. He stepped down from the boardwalk and strode courageously towards the hired gunman.

Garner grimaced. He expected to hear the street rock with the sound of Davis's gun. But to the young gambler's surprise there was no shot.

For some reason Sol Davis was allowing Klondike Casey to approach him.

Garner glanced around the edge of the trough and watched as Casey reached the vicious gunman. Casey stopped a yard away from Davis.

Each man stared into the other's eyes.

'What in tarnation are you doing, Sol?' Casey asked through a cloud of cigar smoke. 'Are you loco? You've earned your money. Why are you wasting lead on that poker player?'

Davis grinned.

'This is personal, Klondike,' he replied. He glanced over his shoulder in anticipation of Garner making the mistake of showing himself. 'That cardsharp owes me and I intend collecting.'

'You should be in your bed, Sol,' Casey said. 'There ain't no profit in killing folks if you don't collect a tidy sum in the process.'

Davis was defiant. 'I've killed the two *hombres* you hired me to kill, Klondike. I even killed their guards. This is my business. Personal business.'

Casey shrugged and poked his cane into the dust. 'I just thought that maybe you might be pushing your luck. There ain't no law in Chandler Crossing but there are a lot of goldminers. There ain't nothing they like better than hanging folks. You being a stranger might be real harmful to your health, Sol.'

Davis lowered his weapon. His scarred face twisted in anger.

'Listen up,' he growled. 'I done your dirty work for you just like we agreed. This ain't nothing to do with you, Klondike. If them goldminers put a rope around my neck I'll surely tell them who hired me. Savvy?'

'I understand only too well, Sol.' Klondike Casey nodded. He smiled, turned on his heel and walked back towards the porch. Davis watched the gambler, who was twisting his swagger stick nonchalantly as he walked. Casey had hired him to kill Wheeler and Dover to enable him to take over their vast business interests.

From his cramped sanctum Garner stared in disbelief at the two very different men. Although the young gambler had not been able to hear one word of their exchange, Garner was convinced that Davis and Casey were connected in some way.

Garner watched as the famed gambler stepped up into the shadows and then seemed to vanish from view as mysteriously as he had appeared. He looked back to where Davis remained standing, as rigid as a statue.

Noting that Davis's attention appeared to be distracted by whatever he and Klondike Casey had been discussing the young poker player decided to take the biggest gamble of his entire life. At stake was his most valuable possession.

His life.

Defying his pain Garner leapt to his feet and swiftly fired his six-shooter at the hired gunman. In as many seconds he had fired his .45 three times, sending the pitiful remnants of his ammunition towards Davis. The air around the young gambler was dense with choking gunsmoke.

Garner lowered his gun and waited for the smoke to clear enough for him to see whether his gamble had paid off.

There was no point in taking cover any longer, Garner reasoned. If he had missed his target he was doomed and he knew it.

The smoke slowly cleared from around the trough. The young gambler took a sharp intake of breath as his eyes focused on the spot where he had seen Sol Davis standing only moments before. He looked from side to side, but there was no sign of the professional killer he had tried to shoot.

'This ain't good,' he muttered. He pushed his six-shooter back into its holster, stepped away from the trough and looked around the moonlit street. He hurt too much to be scared. 'Why don't you damn well shoot and get this over with, Davis?'

'At last I got the big-mouth poker player exactly where I want him.' The chilling voice of Sol Davis cut through the silence and caused Garner to look over his shoulder. 'I'm gonna plumb enjoy killing you.'

The ominous voice had come from the shadows between two stores. Garner raised both his hands in anticipation of his forthcoming execution.

'I do kinda poke my nose into your business, don't I?' Garner said with a shrug. 'I reckon it's too late to apologize, huh?'

'It sure is, Garner,' Davis said. There was bitterness in his tone as he stepped from the shadows and walked up to his defenceless prey.

Garner was about to speak when Davis cocked his gun and raised it to the gambler's face. The brutal killer ran his thumbnail along his scarred features and gave a hideous grin.

'Any last words?' Davis asked his latest victim. 'This is your last chance to say something, Garner.'

Ben Garner felt the barrel of the gun press even more deeply into his cheek. The gambler looked at the face of the hired killer and felt his heart start to pound inside his chest.

'Only one, Davis,' he answered.

'Spill it, Garner. What's the word you wanna tell me?'

'Help?' Garner tried to smile too, but it was impossible. He closed his eyes and waited for the explosive reply to erupt from the six-shooter.

The gambler's misplaced humour was like water off a duck's back to the hired gunman. It meant nothing. Sol Davis narrowed his eyes and gritted his teeth as his finger curled around his trigger.

'*Adios*, cardsharp,' Davis hissed.

Chandler Crossing rocked as the deafening sound of gunfire echoed off the walls of every building.

FINALE

A hundred unseen eyes watched from behind lace curtains as the figure of a man twisted and fell helplessly to the ground at his foe.' The echoes of the shot reverberated off every building along Front Street and the echoes continued long after the dust had settled around the stricken victim.

Ben Garner opened his eyes and looked down.

The startled expression upon his face slowly changed to a smile as it eventually dawned upon the injured gambler that somehow Sol Davis was lying dead. Garner lowered his arms and bent over. He poked the body cautiously and then saw the pool of blood spreading out from beneath Davis's carcass.

Garner straightened up and rubbed his

bemused face.

'How the hell did that happen?' he asked the night air.

The question had barely left his lips when he heard the tapping of a cane on the boardwalk to his left. Garner turned his head and watched as the familiar form of Klondike Casey stepped out from the shadows and strolled towards the injured gambler.

Garner gasped as he saw the smoking gun in Casey's right hand as the older man placed his cane over his shoulder with his left. Klondike Casey kept walking until he was standing over the dead body. Then he holstered his .45 and handed his cane to Garner.

'Hold this, boy,' he gruffed.

Garner held on to the stick as Casey knelt and turned the bloody body over on to its back. Without any hint of revulsion the older man slid his hand into the jacket's pocket and produced a wallet.

Casey stood up and opened the wallet. He withdrew a wad of banknotes and then dropped the empty wallet on to the bloody body.

'What in tarnation is going on here, Klondike?' asked Garner.

Casey raised his eyebrows, took his cane and proffered the inch-thick stack of bills to Garner.

'This is yours, Garner,' he said. He wiped his fingers on a handkerchief and then tossed it on to Davis's face.

Garner looked stunned as he gazed at the money in his hands.

'This is Sol Davis's money, Klondike.'

The older gambler rested on his cane and looked at the dishevelled Garner. He shook his head.

'That's your poker winnings,' Casey told him.

'How do you know?'

Casey raised his eyebrows. 'I should know. I paid Davis with it shortly after he arrived in town.'

Ben Garner's eyes widened. 'Where'd you get it from, Klondike?'

Casey smiled. 'My apologies, Garner. When you won the big pot at the poker game you kinda forced my hand. I had to use that money to pay Davis what I owed him. If I'd won I would not have paid that young girl to lure you into the alleyway.'

Garner rubbed the back of his head. 'You hit and robbed me so you could pay Davis to kill those dudes for you?'

Klondike Casey grinned and turned to walk

back towards the shadows. He glanced over his shoulder and smiled at the confused young gambler.

'I repaid my debt to you, didn't I?' He laughed.

Garner nodded. 'You sure did.'

On the following afternoon Ben Garner had only just managed to rise from his bed when he heard a gentle knocking on his door. He pulled his pants on, then unlocked the door. There stood the beautiful female. Molly Walker was dressed for travelling even though the train was not scheduled to leave for Laredo until after sunset.

'It's about time you woke up,' Molly scolded him. 'I've been knocking on your door for ten minutes.'

Garner sighed as she barged passed him. 'I had me a few tussles last night after I left you in your room, Molly.'

'I heard all about it, Ben.' She sat on the corner of his bed while he continued to get dressed. 'There's a rumour that you actually killed the hired assassin.'

Garner smiled. 'There is, huh?'

'Who really killed Sol Davis?' she asked, a little grin playing on her lips.

'Not me,' he admitted.

Molly Walker watched him find a clean shirt and put it on. Garner strapped his shoulder holster on, then picked up his bloodstained frock-coat and discreetly patted his swollen wallet in its inside pocket. Although he no longer needed the generous fee she had promised him, he could not think of a valid reason not to travel to Laredo with this beautiful woman. As Garner hastily pulled his boots on he noticed her disapproval of his battle-worn garment.

'I'll buy myself a new coat in Laredo,' Garner told her.

Molly Walker studied the man she had chosen to protect her. Even though he was battered and bruised she knew she had chosen wisely.

'Do you want to know what the valuable item I'm hiring you to guard actually is, Ben?' she asked. 'Aren't you the slightest bit curious?'

'Nope.' Garner began buttoning his shirt. 'You don't have to tell me anything, Molly. I'll be on the night train to Laredo with you. Whatever happens, I'll protect you.'

The beautiful female rose to her feet as Garner finished dressing. Her perfume filled his nostrils as she brushed passed him.

'Are you hungry, Ben Garner?' she asked. Her gloved hand turned the doorknob. 'I think we have plenty of time for a good meal before we need to catch the train.'

'I have to buy a box of bullets first.' Garner picked up his hat and watched as she opened the door. He trailed her into the corridor. 'Then we can eat.'

Smiling, Molly turned and pulled a $1,000 bill from her purse. She handed it to him.

'Before I forget, you'd better take this. This is your fee.'

'Much obliged.' Garner accepted the perfumed bank note and watched her walk towards the top of the stairs. She had a graceful motion when walking. Her bustle swayed seductively beneath the layers of her dress.

The gambler raised an eyebrow and loosened his collar.

'I might not know what it is you're taking to Laredo on the night train, Molly,' Garner said. 'But I've got myself a pretty good idea where it's hiding.'